WELCOME TO
GROSSVILLE

WELCOME TO
GROSSVILLE

ALICE FLEMING

CHARLES SCRIBNER'S SONS · NEW YORK

Library of Congress Cataloging in Publication Data
Fleming, Alice Mulcahey, date
Welcome to Grossville.
Summary: The summer after his parents divorce
and he has to move to a less affluent neighborhood,
eleven-year-old Michael copes with learning the true
meaning of friendship and finding new values in his
rapidly changing life.
1. Children's stories, American. [1. Friendship—
Fiction. 2. Moving, Household—Fiction] I. Title.
PZ7.F5993We 1985 [Fic] 84-23664
ISBN 0-684-18289-0

1 3 5 7 9 11 13 15 17 19   F/C   20 18 16 14 12 10 8 6 4 2

Printed in the United States of America.

To Ruth Kinkade

Mom and Dad told me and Jenny one Sunday morning. It wasn't my idea of a great way to wind up a pancake breakfast, but I think they wanted to tell us together, and Dad happened to be home that Sunday. It was the first weekend in months that he wasn't off on a business trip to Chicago or Atlanta. He'd been doing a lot of traveling lately. Mom said it couldn't be helped, but Jenny and I hated it. The house didn't feel right when Dad wasn't around.

I never realized that he might have been staying away on purpose until that Sunday morning, when we were all together at the dining-room table. I had just polished off a big stack of pancakes and had washed them down with a glass of milk.

1

"You've got a milk mustache," Jenny giggled.

I wiped it away with the back of my hand and waited for Mom to say, "Use your napkin, Michael." But Mom wasn't paying any attention to me. She was staring down at her empty plate and running her fingers absentmindedly along the edge of her placemat. All of a sudden, she looked up and cleared her throat.

"Michael and Jenny," she said, "your father and I have something to tell you."

"Your father?" Why so formal? Why didn't she call him Dad or Daddy like she usually did? I sat up and listened closely.

Don't ask me what they said. I only remember bits and pieces of the conversation, but I remember noticing how unreal it all sounded. They talked as if they'd memorized their lines. There was a lot of stuff about mommies and daddies not loving each other any more and about married people having differences that kids don't understand.

What it all added up to—the bottom line, as Dad would say—was that the two of them were getting a divorce. Bombshell Number One.

Bombshell Number Two came later. Another set of memorized lines. Only this time, Mom recited them all by herself. Dad had loaded everything he owned into a U-Haul trailer and had moved to an apartment in New York City.

"Now that your father and I are living apart. . . ," Mom began.

The bottom line on that one was that we were going to move.

"Move?"

"Live somewhere else," she explained.

I knew what she meant. I just couldn't believe she meant it. *Michael Bailey, 28 Forest Road.* That was my name and address. The only address I'd ever known. Could Mom seriously consider changing it? Evidently she could.

"It would cost a lot of money to go on living in Glenville," Mom explained. "And with just the three of us, we certainly don't need this enormous house."

There was no point in arguing; it was already settled. Some people from Ohio were making arrangements to buy our house.

"The father has just been transferred to New York," Mom said. "If everything goes according to plan, they'll be moving in around the first of July."

Jenny did what I felt like doing. She hurled herself down on the floor and screamed her brains out. "I don't *want* to move! I don't *want* to move!" she kept bawling.

You can get away with that when you're eight. When you're eleven, you have to act dignified. I marched out of the room, stomped upstairs, and flushed my pet turtle Lenny down the toilet.

Mom never said a word about Lenny. I suspect she didn't even notice he was missing. A lot of things sailed past her after Dad moved out. For instance, Jenny and I took a quart of chocolate chip ice cream out of the freezer one afternoon and ate it up all by ourselves. Mom has always had a head like a computer when it comes to remembering what's in the freezer, but this time she drew a blank.

"I don't see any chocolate chip ice cream," she remarked as she was checking the food supply one day. "I'll have to put it on my shopping list."

The one thing I was praying Mom would forget was m——. (Jenny and I agreed that if we didn't say the word, it might not happen.)

"Do you think it's working?" Jenny hissed, tiptoeing into my room one night when Mom thought we were both asleep.

"She hasn't said anything more about it," I hissed back. "Maybe that guy from Ohio didn't get transferred to New York after all."

Jenny was rooting for an even bigger miracle. "Maybe Mommy and Daddy will change their minds about the divorce."

I shook my head glumly. "Not a chance."

I knew because I'd already consulted Gary Wilson, the neighborhood expert on the subject. His parents had gotten divorced three years ago.

"You always think they're going to change their minds," Gary told me with a sigh, "but they never do."

"Do you think it's our fault?" I said. "Jenny's an awful brat sometimes, and I can be pretty rotten, too."

"Nah," Gary snorted. "Kids don't have anything to do with it. It's some kind of grown-up trouble that gets them."

Mom had some good news for us at dinner the next night. At least she thought it was good news. "The house is sold," she announced. "The closing's set for June twenty-ninth."

"That's not my idea of good news," I muttered.

I looked across the table at Jenny. Her lower lip was quivering and there were tears in her eyes, but instead of crying, she stuck her thumb in her mouth, grabbed a handful of her hair, and started twisting it slowly around her fingers. I hadn't seen her do that since she was in kindergarten.

Mom plowed right on in that phony upbeat voice she'd developed to tell us things we didn't want to hear. "I've got a million chores to do at the moment," she said. "But as soon as I can spare the time, we'll drive over and take a look at our new home."

"We've already got a home," I reminded her. "We don't need a new one."

"Stop that, Michael! You'll upset Jenny," Mom snapped.

Me upset Jenny? Mom had already done a good job of that on her own.

I sat there brooding about the cold-blooded way in which our own mother was wrecking our lives. She seemed to think that we could pack up and leave 28 Forest Road just like that. No mention of all the other things we'd be leaving—the playroom in the attic, the climbing tree in the yard, the mantelpiece where we hung our stockings on Christmas Eve. Mom obviously didn't give a hoot about those. Moving was the only thing on her mind. She went on such a closet-cleaning, carton-packing, what-can-we-give-to-Goodwill kick that I took to hiding out at my friend David Spencer's house to avoid the confusion.

One afternoon Mom tracked me down there. "Jenny and I are going to see the new house," she said on the other end of the phone. "I thought you'd like to join us."

David lived so close I could have been home in two minutes, but I dawdled. By the time I showed up, Mom and Jenny were already in the car. We couldn't go into the house, Mom explained as she backed out of the driveway. The people we were buying it from were still living there, and we didn't want to disturb them. But at least we could see the outside and take a look at the neighborhood.

We rode for a long time before Mom pulled off the parkway. She turned onto a road lined with gas stations and fast-food joints. I knew we were in trouble when she turned off that into a neighborhood full of boring-looking houses on puny patches of grass. Mom slowed down in front of one of them.

"This is it," she said. "Isn't it charming? Small houses are cozy, don't you think?"

Small? Gimme a break! What we were looking at was a slightly bigger version of the houses in my Monopoly set. Ridiculous. The garages in Glenville were twice as big as that stupid house!

Jenny peered out the car window. She knew there was something wrong with the house, but she wasn't sure what it was. "Are we still in Glenville?" she asked.

"No," Mom said. "This is Humboldt."

Humboldt was the city right next to Glenville. Some parts of it were okay, I guess, but I couldn't imagine why anyone would want to live there. It was full of grimy factories and run-down houses and junky stores. Gross, to say the least.

"Looks like a dump to me," I growled. "And who wants to move to Humboldt anyway? That's Grossville, as far as I'm concerned."

"Don't be so negative, Michael," Mom said. She always said that.

As if moving to a midget house wasn't bad enough, the

stuff from our house in Glenville suddenly began to disappear. First there was Dad's rolltop desk with the old-fashioned swivel chair.

"Your father wanted it for his apartment," Mom explained.

Then the dining-room furniture.

"It's much too big for the new house. We'll only have a dining area."

And what about the glass lamp stuffed with seashells that belonged on the chest in the upstairs hall? Come to think of it, the chest was missing, too.

"There won't be room for all our things, so I had a tag sale," Mom said. "It was that weekend when you and Jenny were out on Long Island visiting Grandma."

A tag sale. What a sneaky trick. And did Mom even apologize for it? No way. If anything, she was proud of herself for selling off our possessions to strangers.

"I made enough money to pay for the move," she boasted.

To make matters worse, she was still acting as if moving to a five-room box in Grossville was the neatest idea since color TV.

"The new house will be a lot easier to clean," she said. "I won't need Ivy to help with the housework."

"But I like Ivy," I protested. "We talk baseball together."

Mom ignored me. "And there's no property to speak of," she went on, "so we won't need Fred to take care of the yard."

I hated to see the moving van pull up in front of 28 Forest Road. School had closed a few days earlier so half the kids in the neighborhood were on hand to watch.

"There goes Michael's bed," I heard one of them say as two men came out toting my captain's bed.

The next time I saw it, they were carrying it up to my room in Grossville.

The new room was half the size of my old room. The furniture looked jammed in, and you had to squeeze between the bed and the dresser to get to the closet.

The movers had brought in my stuff first, and Mom had already unpacked the cartons full of my clothes and toys. My slicker and warm-up jacket were hanging next to each other in the closet right up against my down parka, which was stashed away in plastic for the summer. My Louisville Slugger was propped up in one corner, and my soccer ball and roller skates were on the floor.

But something was missing. What was it? The big red and white fire engine that Dad had bought me for being a good boy when Mom was in the hospital having Jenny. It had been in the back of my closet in Glenville all these years. Now it was nowhere to be seen.

I raced downstairs shouting, "Somebody stole my fire engine!"

Mom took the news calmly. "You haven't played with that fire engine since you were six years old," she said.

"I don't care," I said. "It's *my* fire engine and I want it."

"I'm sorry," Mom said.

She didn't have to say any more. I knew what had happened to my fire engine. She'd sold it to somebody in that dumb tag sale.

I knew I was too big to cry, but I burst into tears anyway. I couldn't help it. In between the sobs, I screamed at Mom with all my might.

"I hate you! I hate you! And I hate Grossville and this

8

rotten stinking midget house. I want to go back to Glen-ville!"

I tore out of the living room and raced upstairs, still sobbing and screaming for all I was worth. I ran into my room, slammed the door, and threw myself face down on the bed.

Mom had come upstairs behind me. She tiptoed in and sat on the edge of the bed. "Poor Michael," she said, gently stroking the back of my neck. "Poor Michael."

After a while my sobs died down. When I turned over and sat up, I was startled to see that Mom's eyes were filled with tears. More tears were rolling down her cheeks.

"Oh Michael," she sobbed, grabbing me and giving me a ferocious bear hug. "I'm sorry. I really am."

If I hadn't been thrown for a loop by the way she was acting, I would have asked her what she was sorry about. Was she apologizing for selling my fire engine? Or for making us move? Or could it be that she didn't like leaving Glenville any more than I did?

I knew I'd hate Grossville, and I was right. The houses looked even dinkier than they had the first day we drove over there. The whole place was tacky compared to Glenville. But like it or not, there I was.

The day after we moved in, I took my bike out of the garage and went looking for someone to play with. I rode up and down several streets without spotting anyone. Then I turned into another, wider street and saw a red brick building at the end of the block. When I got a little closer, I noticed the sign on the front: WOODYCREST INTERMEDIATE SCHOOL. So that was where I'd be going in September.

I wasn't impressed. The building looked grungy, and

the flagpole on the lawn needed a coat of paint. The teachers were probably gross-outs, too.

Four kids about my age were kicking a soccer ball around the playground. I stopped to watch, figuring once they saw me they'd invite me to join the game. Three of the kids were about average, but there was one—a tall kid—who was really good. I'm not bad myself. If we were on the same team, we could work out some good plays.

Before long, the tall kid spotted me. He said something to the others—I couldn't hear what it was—and they all strolled over to where I was standing. I was about to give them a friendly hello when the tall kid snarled, "Don't you know it's rude to stare?"

He sounded like a gangster in some old TV movie. The other three kids could have been his goons.

"I'm sorry," I said. "I was just watching you guys play soccer."

Public Enemy Number One nodded as if I'd finally admitted that I was the rat who'd squealed to the cops.

"You're new around here, aren't you?"

I nodded. "We just moved here from . . ."

He wasn't interested in the details. "I suppose you think you're cool because you've got a ten-speed bike and you're wearing that alligator shirt."

I don't know why I'd think that. All my friends in Glenville had ten-speed bikes and wore alligator shirts. I wondered what this guy had against them.

"Aw, leave him alone, Kevin," one of the goons said. "Let's get back to the game."

Kevin glared at me for another few seconds. The

standard gangster glare. Then he turned on his heel and walked away. "Let's go, guys," he snapped to his goon-squad. "Andy, you be the goalie this time."

I felt like running after him and punching him out, but that wouldn't have been too smart. He was bigger than I am, and if his goons came to his rescue, it would be four against one. The only thing I could do was hold my ground for a few more minutes to show them I wasn't chicken.

My encounter with Kevin killed my interest in any further forays around the neighborhood. I decided to go home and play Pac-Man with Jenny.

As I cruised down the street, a horrible thought crossed my mind. The guys in the playground were the only kids I'd seen in my travels. Suppose they were the only kids my age in the entire neighborhood. Wouldn't that be a bummer?

I was in a foul mood by the time I pulled up to our house. I felt even worse when I saw Jenny and another little girl huddled over a pair of Miss Piggy coloring books on the breezeway steps. They were sharing a box of crayons and yakking away as if they'd known each other for years.

Jenny looked up when she heard the clatter of my kickstand. "Hi, Michael," she said. She turned to her friend. "This is my brother Michael," she said in a super-polite grown-up voice. "Michael, I'd like you to meet my new friend Pamela. She lives across the street."

I'm so much better than Jenny at practically every-thing, it killed me to think that she'd beaten me at friend-finding.

"It didn't take you long to track down someone to play with," I muttered.

Jenny didn't think that was such a remarkable feat. "Pamela likes Miss Piggy, too," she explained.

Pamela smiled shyly and sat there looking pleased with herself.

"Look, Michael," Jenny said, holding up her coloring book to show me the picture she had just finished. "Didn't I do a beautiful job?"

"It looks pretty ugly to me," I snarled. "You made Kermit orange instead of green. Who ever heard of an orange frog?"

I stepped over Pamela's coloring book, marched through the breezeway and into the house. Along the way I felt one of Jenny's crayons crunch beneath my foot.

"Mom-m-m-m-my!" I heard her wail as I headed for my room. "Michael says my picture is ugly! And he doesn't like my Kermit! And he stepped on my orange crayon! And he didn't say hi to Pamela!" She began to cry.

Needless to say, I got a lecture from Mom about my behavior. It ended with me telling Jenny I was sorry and replacing her smashed crayon with one from my box. That was no sweat. I'm not into coloring anymore.

I had a feeling Mom knew what was bugging me because later that evening she said, "There must be plenty of kids your age around here, Michael. Hang in. You'll find them sooner or later."

If she was trying to make me feel better, it didn't work.

"I still don't understand why we had to move to Grossville," I grumbled. "I know other kids whose parents got divorced and none of them moved away."

"A few of them did," Mom reminded me. "Remember the Stickneys? Mrs. Stickney took an apartment in the city. And the McCabes? They moved to Boston where their grandparents live."

"What about Gary Wilson?" I said.

"We're not in the same league as the Wilsons," Mom said. "Mrs. Wilson got a very generous settlement after their divorce, and she also has a great deal of money in her own name."

"And you don't?"

"I'm afraid not," Mom said. "We're going to have to manage on your father's support payments until I can get my act together and find a job."

Bombshell Number Three. How much more did she expect me to put up with?

That night I dreamed I was in Glenville. David Spencer's house is back-to-back with ours, and I was taking my usual shortcut through the azalea bushes that separate our yards. David was calling to me to hurry up and come over, but the azaleas were overgrown and I kept losing my way. It was a crazy dream because in real life the bushes aren't thick, and you couldn't possibly get lost.

I didn't feel too great when I woke up, and I felt even worse when I came down to breakfast and discovered that Jenny's new buddy Pamela had invited her on a picnic.

"She doesn't waste any time, does she?" I snarled. "The little brat must be desperate for friends."

Mom gave me a dirty look, but the crack sailed right past Jenny. She was preoccupied with deciding what to wear—her blue shorts with the white top, or her white shorts with the blue top.

14

"Don't women ever think of anything but clothes?" I sighed.

"Don't be so negative, Michael," Mom said. "Who threw a fit when the shoe store didn't have Adidas in your size?"

"That's different," I told her.

I had finished my orange juice and cereal, and Jenny was still debating what to wear.

"I can't stand any more of this," I said, pushing my chair away from the table and stomping out the door. I didn't have any particular destination in mind, but another bike ride seemed like a good idea. Only this time, I wasn't going anywhere near the Woodycrest School.

I pedalled along for several blocks, keeping my eyes peeled for some action. The only kids I saw were a teenaged girl grooving on the music that was coming through her headset and a little kid trailing a wooden wagon. After a while, I came to a street that intersected with the highway. There was a shopping center on my side of the road, so I parked my bike and killed some time wandering around the stores. I bought a candy bar and a package of gum before retrieving my bike and starting home.

I had just turned into our street. In fact, I was only a block or so from our house when a voice shouted, "HALT!"

Before I knew what was happening, a gang of kids jumped out from behind some high hedges. Quick as a flash, they formed a human chain across the sidewalk, blocking my path and forcing me off my bike. The ring leader was none other than my old friend from the school playground, Public Enemy Number One, also known as Kevin.

"Toll booth," Kevin announced in an official tone.

"You've got to give us fifty cents or we won't let you pass."

"Suppose I don't have fifty cents?"

"Then we beat you up and take your bike."

He sounded as if he was looking forward to it.

Turning to his goonsquad, Kevin said, "How about it, guys—wouldn't you like to have this fancy ten-speed bike? We could all take turns riding it."

Fat chance, I thought to myself. It would always be Kevin's turn.

If I hadn't just spent my last fifty cents on candy and gum, I might have given it to him. I would have felt like a wimp, but at least I'd be out of his clutches. Since I was broke as well as outnumbered, I had to rely on brainpower.

David Spencer and I used to talk for hours about what we'd do if we ever met a mugger. We agreed that karate was the best tactic, but since all we knew about it was what we'd seen on TV, it might be better to use our wits.

So far, neither one of us had run into any muggers, but Kevin was the next best thing. I decided to try out one of the tricks we'd dreamed up. If it didn't work, I knew I'd go limping home with a bloody nose and no bike. But as far as I could see, I was going to do that anyway.

Here goes nothing, I thought. Crossing my fingers and taking a deep breath, I shouted, "Look at that house over there! It's on fire!"

Kevin and his goons spun around to look. The instant they did, I whipped my bike in the opposite direction, hopped back on, and sped off.

If I ever saw David Spencer again, I'd have to tell him how well our trick worked. Public Enemy Number One and his goons stood there trying to figure out where the fire was just long enough for me to get a good head start. By the time it dawned on them that they'd been outwitted, it was too late to chase me. I looked back over my shoulder and saw them standing in a clump on the sidewalk, glaring at my back.

That was a neat trick, I thought, as I whizzed around the block and headed home. There was only one drawback: from now on, I wouldn't be able to leave the house without a bodyguard.

I didn't tell Mom about my run-in with the local mobsters. If she hadn't been so harried, she would have noticed that I'd given up hunting for kids to play with and was sticking close to home.

Now that Dad wasn't around, Mom had to figure out how the fuse box worked and what to do when the toilet didn't flush. I wandered into the bathroom one day and found her attacking a faucet with a pair of pliers. *The Woman's Book of Home Repairs* was propped on the sink beside her.

"I'm not going to pay some plumber a fortune to fix this dripping faucet," she announced. "All it needs is a new washer. I can do that myself."

On top of taking over Dad's chores, Mom had quite a lineup of her own. There was no more Ivy to do the laundry and cleaning and start dinner if Mom was out playing tennis or shopping.

Mom also spent a lot more time worrying about money. I don't remember her pinching pennies or carrying on about high prices when we lived in Glenville. Now she fussed over every cent. What a drag.

Between one thing and another, it took Mom a few days to notice that I was becoming the world's champion stay-at-home. The light clicked on one morning—when she looked up from the grocery list she was frowning over and caught me poking my finger into a jar of peanut butter.

"That's not very sanitary, Michael," she scolded. "Use a knife."

There wasn't much point in hunting for a knife then. I'd already fished out a blob. I licked it off and put the jar back on the shelf, helped myself to a fistful of Oreos, and returned to my regular post in front of the TV.

"Michael! Come back here!" Mom called sharply from the kitchen.

Why was she using that tone? As far as I knew, I hadn't done anything wrong.

I scurried back and found Mom standing by the stove with her hands on her hips, glaring.

"What's the matter?" I asked.

"I just realized something," Mom said. "Every time I see you, you're eating."

"Maybe that's because you usually see me at meal-times," I suggested innocently.

Mom's glare got fiercer. I guess she didn't think my remark was amusing. "That's not what I mean," she said sternly. "I mean stuffing yourself with peanut butter and Oreos in between meals."

"It was just a snack," I protested. "I was hungry."

I was going to remind her that I was a growing boy, but I had a feeling that wouldn't go over too well either.

"Why don't you go out and play?" Mom said.

"I will," I promised. "In a little while. I'm doing something right now."

What I was doing, of course, was the same thing I'd been doing for days—stalling, finding things to make me look busy so I wouldn't have to venture outside and run the risk of hand-to-hand combat with Kevin.

I looked at reruns of "F Troop" and "Gilligan's Island" that I'd already seen a dozen times. I played every video game I owned. I even suffered through a few rounds of Go Fish with Jenny one afternoon, when Pamela was visiting her cousin.

So far, I'd gotten away with it, but I should have known that it was only a matter of time before Mom got on my case. She may have been distracted, but she wasn't *that* distracted.

The one advantage of having divorced parents, I always figured, was that they'd stop ganging up on you. It didn't work out that way. Mom and Dad couldn't see eye-to-eye on too much else, but they were still in cahoots when it came to Jenny and me. I know because they talked on the phone sometimes, and I lurked outside Mom's bedroom door and listened.

Practically the whole conversation was about us and

how we were "taking it." I heard Mom say that Jenny was adjusting very well. She lowered her voice when she talked about me, so I don't know how she thought I was doing. Not too great, I suspected, especially now that she'd caught me sneaking snacks and was beginning to notice how much time I spent indoors.

We saw Dad once a week. He would show up on Sunday mornings and take Jenny and me into New York for the day. Our first stop would be his new apartment. It always looked vaguely familiar, mostly because it was furnished with bits and pieces of stuff he had taken from our house in Glenville. Jenny and I would make a ritual of opening and closing his rolltop desk and spinning around in the old-fashioned swivel chair before he dragged us off for the day's expedition.

Dad must have spent half the week organizing those Sunday expeditions. He had something planned for every minute of the day.

Gary Wilson had told me that would happen when we were back in Glenville. His father did the same thing. "They're afraid you're mad at them, so they knock themselves out taking you places and buying you meals," Gary had said.

If that was what Dad was up to, he was wasting his time. I wasn't going to stop hating him no matter how many places he took us.

Sunday came, and Dad pulled up as usual. Jenny and I trotted out and climbed in the car.

"How's everything going?" he said, as we headed for the city. "What have you been doing with yourselves?"

Before I could say, "Nothing," Jenny launched into a

monologue. "I went on a picnic with my new friend, Pamela," she burbled. "And we had bologna sandwiches and hard-boiled eggs and cupcakes . . ."

I'd already heard the menu twice, so I tuned out and started looking at license plates. I only saw two from out of state. One was from Vermont and the other from Utah. When I turned back into the conversation, Jenny was talking about our new house.

"I like it," she was saying. "It's cozy."

That wasn't even original. She'd stolen it from Mom.

Since Jenny can never remember to brush her teeth or tuck in her napkin, I shouldn't have been surprised that she didn't remember how upset she'd been about moving. Still, it was a downer. How would she feel if I'd deserted her?

Dad turned to me.

"What do you think of your new home, Michael?"

I summed it up in one word: "Gross."

"Oh? What's gross about it?"

"Everything," I told him. "I liked our house in Glenville better."

"Well, of course, that was a handsome house, and Glenville is a lovely community," Dad conceded. "But, you know, Michael, we can't always have things the way we want them."

It was the same line he used to hand out in Glenville when I groused about having to do my homework or hang up my clothes.

I went back to looking at license plates. If Dad wanted to continue the conversation, let him figure out what to talk about next.

What he talked about was where we'd have lunch. "It's

such a beautiful day," he said. "I thought we might try one of the sidewalk cafes around Lincoln Center."

He looked over at me to see if I liked the idea. We spend a fair amount of time in New York, but I'd never eaten at a sidewalk cafe.

I didn't let on. "Whatever you say," I shrugged. Why should I give Dad a break?

I pretended to be unimpressed, but it was fun eating outside and watching the crowd go by. We saw a man walking along with a cat on his shoulder and a lady with huge dangly earrings and green hair. You never see people like that in Grossville or Glenville.

We were halfway through lunch and Jenny was still doing most of the talking when Dad coughed in that funny way he has when he's getting ready to say something important.

"Michael," he began, "your mother tells me you're spending a lot of time indoors. . . ."

As I suspected, Mom had been leaking information to him.

"A boy your age needs exercise and fresh air," Dad was saying. "Your mother and I would like to see you playing soccer and softball the way you used to in Glenville. It's not healthy to be hanging around the house."

"Says who?" I muttered.

"Says me," Dad said. "I'm your father. I have a right to talk to you about your behavior."

"You may be my father," I snarled, "but I think you're a stupid jerk! Why should I listen to anything you say?"

In Glenville that would have earned me a smack in the face. Now Dad looked as if I'd smacked *him* in the face. It took him a couple of minutes to recover from the blow.

Dad has always been a pretty cool guy, but when he finally got around to answering me, his voice was shaky and there were dribbles of sweat on his forehead.

"Look, Michael," he said, "I know you're angry at me, and I can understand why. But I wish you'd stop going out of your way to hurt me. You're only going to end up hurting yourself."

Jenny was starting to fidget. I don't know whether she was upset about the way I'd chewed out Dad or itchy because she hadn't gotten to talk for a while.

"Did I tell you about my new friend, Daddy?" she said, looking up from the hot fudge sundae she'd ordered for dessert. "Her name is Pamela."

"Yes, you told me about Pamela," Dad said. "Be careful with that ice cream now. Don't spill any on your dress."

He leaned over and tucked Jenny's napkin into the front of her dress.

"How about you, Michael?" he said, turning back to me as if he'd completely forgotten that I'd just called him a stupid jerk. "Have you found any kids your age in the neighborhood?"

"One or two," I said. I didn't mention that I'd found them but I was hoping they wouldn't find me.

"Michael's new friend is named Kevin," Jenny volunteered. "Kevin Levin."

Good grief, where did she get that idea? Then I remembered. Just before she went off on that stupid picnic with Pamela, I overheard her saying to Mom, "Poor Michael, he hasn't found a friend yet."

"I have too," I said, darting back into the kitchen to defend myself.

"What's his name?" Jenny demanded.

24

"Kevin."

"Kevin what?"

"Kevin Levin."

Okay, it was a lie, but it was really a joke. I didn't have a friend, period, so I couldn't have a friend named Kevin. But more to the point, who could possibly be dumb enough to believe that there was a human being named Kevin Levin? Jenny, that's who. And Dad too, I guess. He looked a little doubtful about the name, but all he said was, "I'm glad to hear you're both making friends. It isn't easy moving to a new neighborhood. But you've always been outgoing kids. I told your mother it wouldn't take you long to fit in."

After lunch, Dad marched us up Columbus Avenue for a visit to the Museum of Natural History. I was still furious with him. Whenever he tried to talk to me, I answered him in as few words as possible. Most of the time, I just grunted. I had three different sounds: one for *yes*, one for *no*, and one for *maybe*.

It was an okay system for letting Dad know I was mad at him, but as the afternoon wore on, I began to see its drawbacks. Dad was the first person I'd seen in the last two weeks who could carry on a decent conversation about baseball, and there I was, refusing to talk to him. I should have thought of that sooner. It was too late to act friendly now.

When we came out of the museum, we sat on the front steps for a while to rest our feet.

"Now what are we going to do?" Jenny demanded.

Dad's plan called for a stroll through Central Park, then dinner at a Chinese restaurant. From there we took a taxi back to his apartment so he could pick up the car and drive us back to Grossville. He pulled up in front of the house and waited for us to unbuckle our seat belts.

"Aren't you going to come in and say hi to Mom?" I asked.

It was the longest sentence I'd spoken to him all day.

"Sorry, I don't have time," Dad said. "I have to be getting back."

It was dumb of me to ask. He and Mom always avoided each other when he took us for the day. Dad stayed in the car and Mom stayed in the house. Gary Wilson had warned me not to get my hopes up. Why did I keep thinking they'd get back together?

Jenny gave Dad a hug and kiss and dashed up the walk. Dad offered me his hand and I shook it half-heartedly. He clapped his other hand on my shoulder and said, "There's something I promised your mother I'd talk to you about."

"Yeah," I said. "What?"

"She's a little worried about the way you've been pigging out on cookies and peanut butter. How about cutting down on the snacks? You don't want to be the only kid in sixth grade with a paunch, do you?"

I gave him one of my *no* grunts and turned to go. But Dad's hand was still on my shoulder.

"One more thing, Michael," he said in a weird croaky voice. "I . . . er . . . I'm sorry. I really am."

He let go of my shoulder, and I followed Jenny into the house. When I got inside, I headed straight for the freezer.

"It's a little late to be sorry, you stupid jerk," I thought as I helped myself to an ice cream sandwich.

"Don't tell me you're hungry," Mom exclaimed from the kitchen doorway.

26

"Starved," I said. "Dad took us to dinner at a Chinese restaurant. The meal was skimpy, and all I had for dessert was a fortune cookie."

Mom looked at Jenny, who had followed us into the kitchen. "Do you want an ice cream sandwich, too?"

Jenny shook her head. I could have strangled her, the little snitch.

"No thank you," she said sweetly. "We had two helpings of everything at dinner and fried dumplings besides. I'm stuffed."

"Don't be such a wimp," one half of my mind sneered at me. "You can't stay in the house forever. Go ahead and duke it out with Kevin. So what if he is bigger than you are? You're a good fighter. If you caught him alone, you could pound the stuffing out of him."

"But he's never alone," the other half of my mind argued back. "And besides, I'm new around here. People are supposed to be nice to new kids, not go around beating them up and threatening to steal their bikes."

"Were you nice to new kids in Glenville?"

There was no easy answer to that question. Sometimes we were; sometimes we weren't. It all depended on the kids. If a new guy struck us as a nerd or a weirdo . . .

I sat up straight in bed. Did Kevin think I was a nerd or a weirdo? What a crazy idea. Why would he think that?

"Michael!"

My dialogue with myself was interrupted by Mom calling from the foot of the stairs. "Are you ever going to get out of that bed? I want to make it before I go off to do my errands."

"I'm up," I called back, hopping out of bed and scampering into the bathroom. When I came out, Mom was standing in the middle of my room, dressed to go out. "I have an idea," she said.

On a scale of one to ten, Mom's ideas are liable to turn up almost anywhere. Some of them—like taking us to Disney World over spring vacation last year—are definitely tens. Others—like selling my fire engine and condemning us to live in Grossville—are zero minuses. Her latest idea wasn't much better. I'd rate it a zero plus.

"It's about time you and Jenny started pitching in around the house," she said in that upbeat tone I'd learned to distrust. "Why don't you begin by making your own bed? You'd have to do it if you went away to camp, you know."

I knew. That was one of the reasons I'd never wanted to go away to camp.

"I don't know how to make beds," I grunted.

Mom dismissed that excuse with a wave of her hand.

"Jenny will show you," she said. "She's got the hang of it. She used to help Ivy all the time."

Before I could think of another out, Mom made a beeline for the stairs. "I'll be back in about an hour," she called over her shoulder. "You and Jenny can hold the fort while I'm gone."

So there I was, stuck with making my own bed. Well, I knew one thing for sure. I wasn't going to ask an eight-year-old to show me how to do it. I tugged at the sheets to smooth them out and stuffed them in at the sides. Then I slapped my pillow a few times to put it in shape and threw the bedspread over the whole thing. The bed looked lumpy, and the spread was on crooked, but considering that this was my first try, it could have been worse.

When I came downstairs, Jenny was sitting at the kitchen table puzzling over the printing on a box of Rice Krispies.

"What's net *w t*?" she wanted to know.

"Net weight," I told her.

"What's that?"

"How should I know?" I said. "How much it weighs when they put it in a net, I guess."

I downed a glass of orange juice, took the box away from Jenny, and poured myself some Rice Krispies.

"Mommy's gone to do some errands," Jenny informed me. "We're supposed to hold the fort till she gets back."

"I know."

"What does 'hold the fort' mean?"

"It means we should answer the phone politely and write down any messages," I told her. "And not open the door to kidnappers or set the house on fire or fool around with her nail polish."

"I only did that once," Jenny pouted. "And that was a long time ago."

"Yes, but you spilled it all over the bathroom rug, and Mom had a fit."

Jenny's lower lip quivered, and she was obviously on the verge of tears.

"Listen, Jenny, I was only teasing," I said quickly. "No-body's perfect. How about the time I ran into the kitchen and bumped into Mom just as she was putting a pan of lasagne into the oven? Remember how it went *splat* all over the kitchen floor? That was pretty messy, too."

Normally, I don't go out of my way to remind people of the dumb things I've done, but this was an emergency. If Jenny had a crying fit, there was no Mom around to coax her out of it. I'd be left with a sobbing female on my hands.

Jenny smiled. She's kind of cute when she smiles. I ought to be nice to her more often, I told myself. It's not her fault that she's found a friend and I haven't. And she is my sister, after all.

I finished my Rice Krispies and made myself some cinnamon toast. It tasted so good that I decided to go for a second helping.

"Are you still eating?"

Mom was standing in the kitchen doorway with her arms full of bundles.

"Still?" I shot back. "I just started."

"And what have you had so far?"

"Orange juice, Rice Krispies, and cinnamon toast."

"How many slices?"

"Four."

"Michael, if you're not careful, you're going to turn into a blimp."

Mom eased her bundles onto the counter and fixed me with her don't-you-dare-talk-back-to-me stare.

"I know one thing," she announced. "You're not staying in this house another minute. Get out there in the fresh air and sunshine and find yourself something to do besides eat. No more excuses. Now, scoot!"

I scooted—but only as far as the breezeway. Technically, I was out of the house. I could smell the fresh air and feel the sunshine.

I plopped myself down on the breezeway steps and brooded about the mess I was in. Mom wouldn't let me stay inside, but after the trick I'd pulled on Kevin, it wasn't safe to go anywhere else. It was going to take a miracle to get me out of this one.

Dad had his own version of Mom's don't-be-so-negative line. "Think positive," he used to say. I was never sure what he meant by that, but I knew it had something to do with trying to solve your problems instead of sitting around complaining about them.

Suppose they couldn't be solved? Dad had an answer to that one, too. "Almost any problem can be solved if you use your ingenuity," he'd tell me.

I put the old brain to work and astounded myself by coming up with an idea.

Jenny was still in the kitchen chatting with Mom. "Come out here a sec," I called in through the screen door. "I want to talk to you about something."

Jenny appeared promptly, slamming the door behind her.

"What?"

"You're not doing anything special," I said. "How would you like a job?"

"What kind of a job?"

"Detective."

Jenny perked up.

"You know that kid Kevin I told you about?" I continued.

"Kevin Levin?" Jenny said.

"Right. Well, I haven't seen him for a while, and I want

32

you to check him out. Find out where he lives and what he does all day."

Jenny looked dubious. "Why can't you do that yourself?" she said.

"I can," I assured her. "But I thought you might like to earn some money."

Just as I figured, money was the magic word.

"Okay," Jenny said, "but how am I going to do it?"

"Ask Pamela," I said. "She must have some big sisters or brothers. They'd know. This isn't a very big neighborhood. There can't be too many Kevins around."

Jenny rushed back inside and pecked out Pamela's number. Ever since she learned to hit the buttons fast enough for the calls to go through, she never misses a chance to use the phone. The screen door slammed again, and Jenny skipped past me. "I have to go see Pamela," she called over her shoulder. "I'll be back soon."

The breezeway was Jenny's favorite hangout, and she had left a bunch of her toys there. I picked up a tattered Dr. Seuss book and leafed through it. I could still remember when I used to stammer over those baby words.

I was just getting to the good part of the story when Jenny returned with Pamela in tow. They had cracked the case in record time. Pamela's older sister, Kathy, babysat for Kevin's younger brother, Paul. Kathy had given them the whole scoop. Not what I'd call high-powered detective work.

"He lives at 256 Maple Avenue," Jenny began.

"That's the house on the corner with the big hedges," Pamela added.

The place I'd met him the day he threatened to beat me up and steal my bike.

Jenny had further details to report. "He spends practically his every waking minute playing soccer and softball over at the school playground."

"Practically his every waking minute" sounded like too many syllables for Jenny to put together. It must have been a direct quote from Pamela's sister.

"What school playground?" I asked, just to be sure there weren't two.

Jenny turned to Pamela. "What school playground, Pamela?"

"The Woodycrest School," Pamela reported promptly. "It's over that way."

She hurled a stubby arm in the general direction of the school.

"Did you find out anything else?"

"He's in fifth grade going into sixth, just like you," Jenny said.

Great. When school started in September, I'd have to show up with a weapon to protect myself.

"That was good work," I said to Jenny. "Speedy, too."

"How much are you going to pay us?" Jenny demanded.

"A dime."

Luckily, I had one in my pocket. When I handed it over, the two girls giggled with delight.

"Can I ask a question?" Jenny said suddenly.

"Shoot."

"Why did you tell me his name was Kevin Levin when it's really Kevin Sherman?"

"I don't know," I lied. "Maybe because I like Kevin Levin better, don't you?"

Pamela did.

"Kevin Levin," she squealed. "Kevin Levin went to

heaven. Kevin Levin comes from Devon. Kevin Levin's only seven."

She and Jenny started jumping around the lawn chanting Kevin Levin rhymes. Some of the words didn't make any sense, but they didn't care.

While my detective team chanted themselves silly, I sat back and congratulated myself. Thanks to my ingenuity, I now had the dope on Kevin's routine. As long as I steered clear of the Woodycrest School, 256 Maple Avenue, and the route between the two, I could venture beyond the breezeway steps without risking my life. That left me a fair amount of territory to roam around in. I was sure I could scare up somebody in the area who wanted to be friends.

"Keep on thinking positive," I told myself as I sauntered inside to see if it was time for lunch. "You might get out of this mess yet."

I knew exactly the kind of kid I wanted for a friend. He had to be the right age and the right grade in school, but above all, he had to be an A–number one, all-American sports nut like me.

That didn't seem like too much to ask. There were plenty of kids in Glenville who filled the bill. David Spencer was special because we both loved the Yankees and hated the Red Sox, and also because we lived so close. But I hung out with other kids besides David. We had a regular gang who lived near each other and were in the same grade in school.

Finding people to play with had never been a problem in Glenville. That's why I was so totally unprepared for what was happening here in Grossville. Now that I'd mapped out a safety zone for myself, though, things were bound to improve. For the first time in days, I was itching to get out of the house. I bolted down my lunch, filched a couple of chocolate chip cookies when Mom wasn't looking, and headed for the door.

If you turned left at the end of our driveway, you'd be heading toward Maple Avenue and the Woodycrest School. I turned right. I walked for three blocks without running into anyone under the age of fifty. The neighborhood seemed to be full of grown-ups fussing over their lawns or doing repairwork on their houses. I was beginning to worry, but since I didn't have anything better to do, I kept on going.

On the very next block, I spotted a kid peering into some bushes in front of a red brick house. He could have been my age or a little younger. It was hard to tell; he was small and skinny, but he had an old face.

I was tempted to stop and ask him what he was looking for, but I was wary after my experience with Kevin. I slowed my pace and pretended to be examining some cracks in the sidewalk.

"Psst!"

I looked over and saw that the kid was smiling at me and motioning to me to come closer. I went bounding across the lawn to see what he wanted.

"There's a family of catbirds in here," he whispered.

"Catbirds?"

He nodded and parted the branches gingerly so I could see what he was talking about. There among the leaves were five baby birds snuggled in a nest. Their eyes were closed, but their mouths were open as if they were waiting for the mother bird to drop in some food. I'm not particularly interested in birds, but this was quite a sight.

"Wow," I said.

The kid grinned approvingly. He seemed eager to make friends. Quite a change from you-know-who. I had a sneaky suspicion that he wasn't my type, but I wasn't about to quibble. At this point in my life, any friend was better than none.

The kid's name was Ralph Kowalski, I found out; and he was in fifth grade going into sixth, just like me. When I told him I was new in the neighborhood, he said, "You must live in Bobby Pagano's old house. I saw the movers unloading your stuff."

I wondered if Bobby Pagano had minded moving as much as I did. In any case, I was happy to hear that someone in Grossville had noticed my arrival.

"We used to live in Glenville," I said, partly to make conversation and partly to establish the fact that I wasn't your average everyday kid.

The mention of Glenville didn't cut any ice with Ralph. If anything, it made him hostile.

"The high income district," he said, putting on a snooty face. "That's where all the country club types hang out."

It had never occurred to me that anyone would have anything against Glenville. I decided to backtrack fast.

"Glenville's not such a ritzy place," I said. "The neighborhood we lived in wasn't much different from this one."

What a lie that was!

Ralph wasn't convinced. "My father says you can't live in Glenville unless you own a Mercedes," he said.

38

"He must have been kidding," I said. "I know lots of people who drive Pintos."

Another lie.

Ralph thought about it for a minute and evidently decided not to hold Glenville against me. "Why don't you come around to the backyard?" he said. "I'll fix us some lemonade."

He led me around the side of the house and into a small, well-tended garden.

"Have a seat," he said, gesturing to a white wooden lawn chair. "I'll be back in a minute."

I sat down and Ralph disappeared into the house. He returned in a few minutes carrying two glasses of lemonade and settled himself in a lawn chair that was a twin of mine.

Ralph was about to take a sip of his lemonade when something at the far end of the garden caught his eye. Reaching for a pair of binoculars that were lying on the arm of his chair, he trained them on what looked like a brand new birdhouse sitting on top of a wooden pole. It was one of those bird apartment houses with three stories and lots of holes. Two birds were perched on the roof; two or three more were poking their heads in and out of the holes.

"Hey," Ralph exclaimed. "It looks like four more purple martins have moved in!"

What the heck were purple martins? They sounded like a rock band.

"They're amazing birds," Ralph went on, still staring through his binoculars. "Do you know they fly all the way up here from Brazil?"

39

I didn't know that. In fact, up until a few seconds ago, I didn't even know that purple martins were birds.

There was no point in faking it. "I'm not big on birds," I confessed. "The only ones I can recognize are the Toronto Bluejays and the Baltimore Orioles."

Ralph grinned. "Have you ever seen a *real* Baltimore oriole?" he said. "We've got a family of them over there in that mulberry tree. Look, there's the father now."

I followed Ralph's finger and caught a glimpse of a black and orange bird flitting through the branches.

"He's wearing the team colors," I said.

It was getting more and more obvious that Ralph wasn't my type, but at least I was learning something. From now on, I'd be able to recognize an oriole when I saw one.

Since I'd already admitted that I didn't know anything about birds, I figured it was okay to ask a stupid question. "How did a bunch of birds get named after a city?"

"They were both named after Lord Baltimore," Ralph informed me. "You know, the guy who founded Maryland. Black and orange were the colors of his family crest."

I'd heard of Lord Baltimore, anyway—but only because we'd studied him in history.

"How come you know so much about birds?" I asked.

"I've got cystic fibrosis and I can't run around very much. Bird watching is a good hobby."

Neither one of us could think of anything to say for a minute, so I broke the silence by asking another stupid question: "What's cystic fibrosis?" I surprised myself by being able to pronounce it.

"It's something you're born with," Ralph explained.

"Nobody knows what causes it, but you get all choked up with mucous and it's hard to breathe."

"Is it like asthma?" David Spencer had that.

Ralph shook his head. "It's worse."

"That doesn't sound too cool," I said.

Ralph shrugged. "You get used to it."

"Do you know a kid named Kevin?" I said.

"Everyone knows Kevin," Ralph said. "He thinks he's the king of the neighborhood."

"Oh yeah?" I said. "Well, if he ever runs for the job, he won't get my vote."

I told Ralph about my run-ins with Kevin.

"Sounds just like him," Ralph said with a knowing look. "Kevin doesn't take kindly to strangers."

"Why not?"

"Because he's the big cheese around here, and he's afraid some new kid will come along and bump him out of first place. Basically, he's very insecure."

"He didn't strike me as insecure," I said. "He acted like he owned the whole world."

"That's just a cover," Ralph explained. "Insecure people are always going out of their way to impress people with how terrific they are."

Good grief, the kid was a psychologist, too!

What he said made me a little uneasy though. I'd gone out of my way to impress Ralph with the fact that I came from Glenville. Did that mean I was insecure?

I asked Ralph if he liked the Yankees. "I don't have anything against them," he said. "But to tell you the truth, I'm not into baseball. I've got too many other things to do."

"Like what?"

"Well, right now I'm making a series of sketches of all the birds I've spotted in this yard. Would you like to see the ones I've finished so far?"

When I said yes, he disappeared into the house and came back with a folder full of pictures. They were so good you couldn't believe a kid had done them.

"Hey!" I exclaimed. "You're a real artist."

"I hope so," Ralph said shyly. "That's what I want to be when I grow up."

"Really?" I said. "I'd like to be a major league pitcher."

I realized it was getting late when Ralph's mother called out the window to tell him to wash his hands, dinner was almost ready. I jumped up and said I had to be going.

"Come around again," Ralph urged. "I'll show you my bird books."

"Sounds good," I said. "Maybe tomorrow."

When I got home, my own dinner was almost ready.

"There you are," Mom exclaimed as I came bouncing in the door. "I was afraid you'd be late."

She didn't ask me where I'd been until we were almost finished eating. Then she said casually, "You've been out all afternoon. Does that mean you found someone to play with?"

"Sort of," I said.

I thought about Ralph, with his interest in birds and his lack of interest in baseball. If I'd met him in Glenville, I would have written him off in no time and gone looking for someone else. Here in Grossville, he struck me as a little bit different but basically a nice guy. Or was that because there wasn't anyone else?

Mom interrupted my thoughts. "Michael, I asked you a question."

"Oh. What?"

"What does 'sort of' mean?"

"I don't know," I sighed. "What's for dessert?"

Since Ralph had gone out of his way to make friends with me, I assumed he was as desperate as I was for someone to play with. I was wrong. He already had a zillion friends; he didn't have to go looking for more.

The reason he had invited me into his yard that first day, I decided, was that he took the same approach to people as he took to birds. He was interested in all of them. When I got to know Ralph better, I asked him if my theory was true.

"I never thought about it that way," he said. "But I guess you're right."

He gave me a cocky grin. "But that's not so terrible, is it? Don't you enjoy meeting different kinds of people?"

I shrugged. If I'd been honest, I would have said, "No. I get along better with kids who are just like me."

That wasn't Ralph's approach at all. His friends ranged in age from a sixteen-year-old named Sam, who knew a lot about woodworking and was helping him build a bird feeding station, all the way down to a six-year-old named Jamie, who grooved on looking through the wrong end of Ralph's binoculars.

There were even a couple of girls who showed up in the Kowalskis' backyard from time to time. Ralph seemed to enjoy their company, but I never knew what to say to them. David Spencer and I didn't play with girls.

When Sam, the sixteen-year-old, was around, there was always a lot of hammering and sawing going on. The rest of the time we played games like Steal the Bacon or Simon Says. Not the sort of thing that would pack them in at the Meadowlands. "Lame games," David Spencer used to call them. I almost hated myself for enjoying them.

The one game I didn't enjoy was Scrabble. One of the girls, Meredith, was a demon player, but even she had a hard time beating Ralph, whose vocabulary ran to words like *junco* and *vireo* that the rest of us had never heard of.

When we challenged him, Ralph didn't hesitate for an instant. "A junco is a type of sparrow," he'd tell us, or, "A vireo is a green and white bird that sings like a robin."

I looked them both up in the dictionary when I got home just to be sure he wasn't putting us on. He wasn't.

I had a good time at Ralph's, but not good enough to make it my regular hangout. I still spent a fair amount of time at home and, as Mom noted somewhat sarcastically, when I was home I was usually in the kitchen.

She caught me there one day scrounging through the cabinets looking for something to eat. The pickings were lean. Mom had stopped buying all sorts of things, like cookies and pretzels, as part of some fiendish plan to keep me from eating between meals.

I'd been thinking of tapering off anyway. My pants were getting a little tight. When I took them off at bedtime you could see where the elastic had cut into my middle. Even so, it annoyed me that Mom had shut off the supply line without consulting me.

"A kid could starve to death around here," I grumbled.

"Not if he helped himself to the carrot and celery sticks on the second shelf of the refrigerator," Mom retorted. "Or had some of those luscious plums I bought yesterday."

"Yuck. No thanks. How about this?" I held up a package of devil's food cake mix that had been hiding at the back of the cabinet behind a jar of spaghetti sauce. "The directions look simple. I'll whip it up right now and we can have it for dessert."

Score one for my side. Mom couldn't think of any reason to object. She showed me where she kept the cake pans and racks, and said, "Follow the instructions carefully, and be sure to clean up the kitchen when you're through."

The cake turned out a little lopsided, but it tasted fine. We had some for dessert, and I polished off the rest the next day. Now that I'd gotten the hang of it, I wanted to keep on going. My next creation was tollhouse cookies. They got burned on the bottom, but not so badly that you couldn't eat them. I was looking around for something else to tackle when Mom intervened. "I'm instituting a new rule," she announced. "Cooking is okay, but you've got to make something besides cakes and cookies."

"How about this recipe for molasses crisps that I found on the back of a cereal box?"

Mom gave me an exasperated stare.

"I mean something that won't result in obesity and rotting teeth," she said. "Something that's made with meat or vegetables and just might be good for you."

I made a face.

"Don't be so negative," Mom said. "Lots of things that are good for you taste good, too."

She reached over and took her copy of *The Joy of Cooking* off the shelf next to the kitchen phone.

"Check out some of the recipes in here," she said, handing it to me. "There ought to be one or two that appeal to you."

"Have you been keeping up your tennis?" Dad asked me the following Sunday, when he and Jenny and I were visiting the Bronx Zoo.

"No," I said.

Dad frowned. "The pro at the club in Glenville thought you had a very promising forehand," he said.

"But we don't belong to the club any more."

Dad ignored the dig. "Your mother tells me there are some public courts not too far from the house," he continued. "Maybe you and your new pal—what's his name? Kevin?—could go over there and play."

"Maybe," I said.

I could just see myself showing up at Kevin's in my tennis outfit. If he was in a good mood, he'd throw mud on my shirt. If he wasn't, he'd bash me over the head with my Prince Junior.

"What shall we look at first?" Dad asked.

"How about the birds?" I suggested. Don't ask me why.

"I didn't know you liked birds," Dad said. "I thought the snakes were more your speed."

Jenny shuddered. "The snakes are creepy," she declared. "Let's go for the birds."

I'd never been in the birdhouse before. It was better than I expected. There were all sorts of tropical birds I'd never heard of, and one of the cages was reserved for the owls. They were alive, but they looked stuffed.

"That's because it's daytime," Dad said. "They're all asleep. Owls are nocturnal birds. They don't get cracking until after dark."

The ugliest of the bunch was a great horned owl. It had a wicked scowl and a head like a tiger. According to the sign next to the cage, great horned owls prey on creatures twice their size. They kill and eat rabbits, ducks, skunks, and even cats, it said.

"Real tough characters, those great horned owls," I said.

If only I knew their secret, I could take on Kevin Sherman. It bugged me that I was still hiding out from that kid. I'd go to bed some nights swearing that I was going to march over to the playground the next morning and duke it out with him. But when morning came, I'd lose my nerve, and it would be back to either of my two regular hangouts—the kitchen or Ralph Kowalski's backyard.

"Your mother tells me you've taken up cooking," Dad said when we finally got tired of the birdhouse and collapsed on a bench outside.

"You guys ought to be working for the CIA," I snorted. "Then you could spy on the Russians instead of on me."

Dad looked hurt.

"I wish you wouldn't refer to it as spying," he sighed. "Your mother knows that I'm very much interested in you and Jenny. We keep in touch because we want to help you weather this difficult period. . . ."

"You mean the divorce?" I don't know why he couldn't call it by its right name.

"Yes."

I suppose it didn't matter what he called it. I didn't want to hear about it anyway. He and Mom obviously weren't going to get undivorced. I wasn't going to escape from Grossville. There wasn't any point in discussing it.

In that case, maybe there wasn't any point in being rotten to Dad anymore either.

That was an interesting thought. I'd been rotten to him for so long I'd almost forgotten that I hadn't always treated him that way. Dad and I used to be good buddies. I wondered if we could be again.

I remembered that day at the sidewalk cafe when I chewed Dad out and called him a stupid jerk. He said that if I didn't stop trying to hurt him, I'd end up hurting myself. That struck me as a lot of hogwash then. Lately, I wasn't so sure. Hating your father can be as miserable for you as it probably is for him.

Dad had told me that day he was sorry about the divorce. He was obviously hoping I'd forgive him. But I'd been holding out, making him squirm. Maybe it was time to give him a break. The problem was: Where should I start?

Think positive, I told myself.

I leaned forward on the bench and gave Dad a friendly smile.

"About the cooking," I said. "Mom says that some of the world's greatest chefs are men."

"She's right," Dad said. "But it's a good idea for boys to learn cooking even if they're not planning to turn pro. I often wish I'd mastered more than the bare essentials—especially now that I'm fending for myself."

"You want a few lessons?" I said. "Here I am."

I don't know why I said that. Too much positive thinking, I guess. I certainly didn't expect Dad to take me up on it. So far I'd tried only one recipe from *The Joy of Cooking* —cole slaw. That hardly made me an expert.

Dad ended the day by taking us to dinner at an Italian restaurant in the Bronx that he knew about. There was a fountain with colored lights in the middle of the dining room, and the waiters were extra nice to kids.

When the check came, Dad shook his head at how much it cost.

"You know, Michael," he said, as he was slipping his credit card back into his wallet. "I might take you up on those cooking lessons. That meal just set us back fifty bucks. We could have a good time and save some money besides if the three of us fixed dinner at my apartment some Sunday."

"The three of us?" I said. "Jenny doesn't know how to cook."

"I do too," Jenny said.

"What can you cook?"

"Toasted marshmallows," she replied smugly.

When Dad used to barbecue steak on the outdoor grill in Glenville, the coals would glow for hours. After dinner,

Mom would get out some long forks and let Jenny and me toast marshmallows.

"That was a long time ago," I reminded Jenny. "And yours always fell off the fork anyway."

"I toasted some over at Pamela's house yesterday and none of them fell off," Jenny said, sticking out her tongue at me.

"Pamela's a fuzzball," I said.

"Cut it out, Michael," Dad snapped. "This is the nicest Sunday we've spent together since your mother and I broke up. Don't spoil it by giving your sister a hard time."

I shut my mouth and didn't say another word against Pamela. Or Jenny either. Dad was right; it had been a nice day. I wasn't going to be the one to spoil it.

If anyone had told me at the beginning of the summer that I'd spend the better part of a Sunday afternoon gaping at birds and—even crazier—enjoying it, I would have written him off as a knucklehead. Then again, if anyone had told me only twenty-four hours ago that I'd stop making nasty remarks about Pamela the first time Dad told me to, I wouldn't have believed that either. I don't know what was getting into me.

I went over to Ralph's the day after our visit to the zoo. I couldn't make up my mind whether to mention the birdhouse or not. If he'd already been there (and chances were he had), he might shut me up with some comment like, "Big deal. Who hasn't done that?"

As soon as I rounded the corner of the Kowalskis' house and saw Ralph with Meredith, I realized that I did want to tell him, only I didn't want to do it with Meredith around. The two of them were sitting at the picnic table playing Scrabble. I was already intimidated by Meredith, and it didn't help that she was wearing a t-shirt that said: We Haven't Come That Far And Don't Call Me Baby!

"Hi, Michael," she said. "What's up?"

"Not much," I mumbled, wishing that girls didn't make me tongue-tied.

Meredith didn't have that problem with boys. "Ralph's beating me again," she complained. "If he wasn't such a good kid, I'd hate him."

I glanced over at the score pad. Meredith wasn't that far behind, but Ralph had just demoralized her by coming up with one of his bird words—towhee.

"Look at that! I can't stand it!" she exclaimed, throwing up her hands. "This is the last time I'm going to play Scrabble with a bird freak!"

"Don't be a sorehead," Ralph chided her good-naturedly. "The game's almost over," he went on, turning to me. "Have a seat. As soon as we're finished, we'll figure out something all three of us can do."

They played the last three letters, and after all her moaning and groaning, Meredith won by five points. With the game over, I was hoping she'd go home. No such luck.

"I made a whole pile of money returning empty soda cans," she said. "Let's go over to The Ice Cream Factory and I'll treat you guys to some cones."

The suggestion made me feel a little friendlier toward Meredith.

Ralph ducked inside to tell his mother where we were going and we set off down the street. I had no idea where The Ice Cream Factory was, but Ralph and Meredith led me to a row of stores just beyond the shopping center. The Ice Cream Factory was right in the middle, and it was packed with customers. Half the people in Grossville must have had the same idea.

Ralph and Meredith said hi to a crowd of kids who had already been waited on and were standing around outside licking their cones.

"They go to our school," Ralph told me. "A couple of them will be in our class next year."

"See that simpy-looking one with the fur head?" Meredith whispered, poking me in the ribs with her elbow. "She's a real pain."

I glanced over and saw a girl with short curly hair that actually did look like fur growing out of her head. From the fuss-budgety expression on her face, I could easily believe she was a pain.

"Meredith says terrible things about people she doesn't like," Ralph explained as we pushed our way in the door and joined the line. "Do you know what she calls Kevin Sherman? Kevin the Killer."

"Speak of the devil," Meredith muttered, giving me another poke in the ribs.

Outside, framed in the plate glass window, stood Kevin himself. He was wearing a New York Yankees cap and had a baseball glove tucked under one arm. Incredible. The guy could have been me in my Glenville days. I wondered for the skatey-eighth time why he'd taken such a hate to me. Couldn't he see that we were two of a kind?

By now Kevin had his hand on the door. The last thing I needed was to have him see me with a girl and a bird-watcher. My image would be ruined for all time. I spun around and stared intently at the list of flavors hanging on the wall. There were twenty-two of them, and I had them almost memorized by the time the kid behind the counter said, "What'll you have?"

Meredith ordered vanilla with chocolate sprinkles, Ralph went for butterscotch, and I was torn between my two favorites—coffee and chocolate chip. I chose coffee, and as I turned away from the counter, I bumped smack into Kevin. I couldn't pretend I didn't see him. There was nothing to do but tough it out and say hi. Ralph gave him a much warmer greeting and Meredith went all-out.

"Hi, Kevin," she bubbled. "I like your baseball cap. Is it new?"

Kevin looked surprised but pleased.

"Yes," he said in a very un-killerlike tone. "I got it at the game last night."

I wanted to say, "The Yanks did all right, didn't they?" but the kid behind the counter was waiting to take his order and Kevin turned away.

"How come you're so friendly with Kevin all of a sudden?" Ralph asked Meredith when we got outside. "I thought you hated him."

"He's not one of my favorite human beings," Meredith replied. "But I was performing a psychological experiment. I wanted to see how he'd act if I went out of my way to be nice to him for a change."

"Now you know," Ralph said. "He was nice back."

Meredith rolled her eyes. "Maybe my mother is right.

She always says you can catch more flies with honey than you can with vinegar."

I wasn't impressed. One friendly remark—and to a girl, at that—didn't prove a thing.

"Mine always says a leopard doesn't change his spots," I grunted.

"And mine always says, don't spill ice cream on your nice clean t-shirt," Ralph chimed in.

"Oops."

Meredith glanced down and scooped up a blob of ice cream that was dribbling down her chest. She rolled her eyes again and went back to licking her cone.

I can't remember what we talked about on the way back to Ralph's, but by the time we got there I was feeling more at ease with Meredith. I decided to bring up the birdhouse.

"My father took me and my sister to the zoo yesterday," I began.

Meredith was interested right away.

"Did you see the llamas?" she wanted to know. "The last time I was there one of them spit at me. Boy, was that yucky!"

"I didn't see them this time," I said. "We spent most of the afternoon in the birdhouse."

"That's always my first stop," Ralph said. "Did you like it?"

"It was neat."

Just as I figured, Ralph had been to the birdhouse dozens of times, but that didn't stop him from wanting to hear about my visit. I couldn't help thinking how different he was—in a nice way—from David Spencer. I remember when we came back from Disney World, every time I tried to tell David about something we'd done there, he'd look bored and cut me off.

"Oh yeah, we did that," he'd say. I got the feeling that he couldn't stand the fact that he wasn't the only one who'd visited Disney World.

"I've never been to the birdhouse," Meredith said. "What have they got that's worth seeing?"

"Everything," I told her. "You'd like the hummingbirds. They're so tiny, and they come in millions of different colors. The sign said there are more than six hundred species."

"I have a book about hummingbirds," Ralph said. "It's got pictures of all of them. You should see the size of the eggs they lay. They look like pearls."

"What else did you see?"

I've never thought of myself as a good talker, but Meredith was hanging on my every word.

"A great horned owl," I said. "What a weird-looking bird that is!"

Ralph nodded. "He's a real killer, too."

"Hmmmm," said Meredith. "The Kevin Sherman of the bird world."

"That's not nice," Ralph scolded. "What happened to your be-kind-to-Kevin experiment?"

"Sorry." Meredith clapped her hand over her mouth. "I forgot."

"That's funny," I said. "The great horned owl made me think of Kevin, too."

"Aw, give poor old Kevin a break," Ralph said. "I know he likes to act like Mr. Tough Guy, but he's really a nice kid when you get to know him."

"Sure," I said. "But how do you get to know him?"

57

That was a pretty crazy question for me to be asking, considering the fact that I'd been hiding out from the guy all summer. Did I want to get to know a mean rotten bully like Kevin Sherman? I knew the answer the second I asked the question: You bet.

Since I don't get too many letters, I don't pay much attention to the mail, but somewhere in the course of an ordinary Wednesday morning, a square white envelope addressed to me appeared on the table in the downstairs hall.

"Looks like an invitation to a party," Mom said.

I couldn't imagine who'd sent it. None of my friends from Glenville have summer birthdays. David Spencer's is in January. I ripped open the envelope and pulled out a card in the shape of an eleven. You're invited to an 11th Birthday Party, it said.

I flipped it open and saw that the party was for Ralph. It was on August 18th at 9 A.M.—an odd hour. Just below the phone number to RSVP, someone had written: Bring your bathing suit!

I tossed the invitation back on the table with a grunt.

"What's the matter?" Mom said. "I thought you liked parties."

"I do," I sighed. "But I don't think I'll like this one."

I could picture the whole scene. There'd be girls and little kids and people lurching around blindfolded trying to pin the tail on the donkey.

"It says, 'Bring your bathing suit,'" Mom pointed out hopefully. "You like to swim."

"Big deal," I snarled.

If we went swimming at all, it would be at that public pool Mom knew about. More likely, we'd get into our bathing suits and Ralph's mother would squirt us with the hose.

"I thought you and Ralph were friends," Mom said.

I didn't answer.

"Well, aren't you?"

"We are and we aren't," I told her.

"You'll have to explain."

I wasn't sure I could, but I took a crack at it. "I guess you could call Ralph a stopgap friend," I said. "He'll do until somebody better turns up."

That wasn't a nice thing to say, but Mom took it better than I expected. "Is there a rule against going to a stopgap friend's birthday party?" she asked.

"I didn't say I wouldn't go. I just don't expect to have a very good time."

"Well, if you go with that attitude, you won't."

I steeled myself for another don't-be-so-negative-

Michael lecture, but Mom surprised me by taking a different tack.

"I've gone to lots of parties that I thought would be terrible and they weren't," she said. "And I've also gone to lots of parties that I thought would be great and I was bored to tears. You never know."

"In this case, I know."

I also knew that I was being totally negative. One reason, I guess, was that I was disappointed. I'd been secretly hoping that the invitation was from somebody else. But, of course, there wasn't anyone else.

I put the party out of my mind and went into the kitchen to look for something to eat. The first thing I saw when I opened the refrigerator door was a glass full of celery and carrot sticks. I shoved it aside and reached for the grape jelly. A few dabs on some graham crackers would be a perfect pre-lunch snack.

"Eating again?" It was Mom.

I could have said, "Spying again?" but I kept my mouth shut.

"Just fixing myself a little snack," I said. "It's been a while since breakfast."

Mom glanced at the clock. "It's been exactly forty-five minutes," she said.

I put the grape jelly back in the refrigerator and slammed the door.

"About the party," Mom said.

"What about it?"

"If you honestly don't want to go, you can simply tell Ralph you're sorry, but you're busy that day."

"But I'm not."

"I know," Mom said. "But those kinds of white lies are designed to get you off the hook without hurting anyone's feelings."

The question was: Did I want to get off the hook? I spent the rest of the day close to home, not actually in the house—Mom wouldn't have tolerated that—but moping around the breezeway or sitting in one of the canvas chairs in the backyard.

I got out my *Baseball Encyclopedia* and killed some time looking up the batting averages of the old-time stars. They had some awfully good hitters back then. Pete Rose is a lightweight compared to Ty Cobb.

I was trying not to think about Ralph's party, but I wasn't succeeding. The worst part was that I didn't know why I was getting worked up about it. I'd been hanging out with Ralph for weeks. Why should I balk at going to his party? Had I finally had it up to here with the cream-puff crowd? Or could it be that I felt guilty about showing up at a guy's party when I was planning to ditch him the minute I found someone better?

If only Mom had issued an order. If she'd said, "Of course you're going. It would be rude not to." Or, "If you really don't like Ralph, you'd be a hypocrite to go to his party."

But Mom was staying out of this. When I came inside for lunch, she didn't even mention the party. All she talked about were the couple next door. I don't know why she found them so interesting. They certainly weren't her type. They were both old and fat and they spent most of their time puttering in their garden. I could hear them through the bushes, and they talked to each other in some foreign language. I don't know what it was.

"Their name is Novotny and they're from Czechoslovakia," Mom told me. "They left in 1968, just before the Russians marched in. They have a daughter who's studying to be a doctor and a son who's married and lives in California."

"How did you find all that out?" I inquired.

"I complimented them on their garden and we got chatting. They told me a little bit about themselves."

A little bit? It sounded like she'd gotten their whole life history.

"They're not like the people you used to hang around with in Glenville."

"True," said Mom. "But you can *like* people even if you're not *a*like. Besides, I'm not exactly hanging around with them. They're neighbors, and they seem like nice people, so why shouldn't we be friends?"

It all sounded perfectly logical, the way things should have been between me and Ralph—and would have been if Kevin Sherman wasn't so hooked on impressing new kids with the fact that he was king of the neighborhood.

"By the way," Mom said, "if you're not doing anything special after lunch, maybe you could help me make pesto. I found some fresh basil at the supermarket yesterday."

Pesto is a yummy green sauce that Mom sometimes puts on spaghetti instead of tomato sauce. I never knew it was made with basil, but I suppose that's why it's green.

I'd be a great chef if every recipe was as simple as pesto. All you do is add garlic, olive oil, Parmesan cheese, and some Italian nuts called pignoli to the basil. You don't even have to cook it. You can do the whole thing in the blender.

Mom washed the basil and assembled the other ingredients, and I manned the blender. In no time at all, we had enough pesto for a half-dozen spaghetti suppers. Only then did it cross my mind that I'd been tricked into making something that Mom would classify as Good For You. Since it happens to taste good, too, I decided not to hold it against her.

"Thanks, Michael. You were a big help," Mom said as she was pouring the last batch into a plastic container. "Now you can run off and do whatever you were planning to do before I dragooned you into helping me."

"I wasn't planning to do anything," I said. "I was just lolling around trying to make up my mind about Ralph's party. What do you think I should do?"

Mom was still cagey.

"Why bother about what I think?" she said. "You're the one who has to live with the decision."

"Yes, but if you were me, what would you do?"

"I don't know. I'm not you," Mom said. Then she relented a little. Maybe she saw that I was really stumped. "It might help you make up your mind if you look at it this way," she said. "If you go, you may not have a very good time, but if you don't go, you'll never know what you missed."

That made sense. Besides, even a so-so party would beat sitting home. At least I could enjoy some ice cream and cake without having to put up with fishy looks or snide remarks about my waistline. So, okay. My mind was made up.

There was no point in phoning Ralph; it would be just as easy to go over and tell him in person. I washed the smell of garlic off my hands and set off for the Kowalskis.

64

As soon as I talked to Ralph, I realized I'd made the right decision. He told me all about the party, and it wasn't going to be anything like I'd imagined. We were going to spend the day at Playland. That's why it was starting at 9 A.M.

Playland is an amusement park with all kinds of fantastic rides. And we were supposed to bring our bathing suits because there's a pool there, too. (I'd seen it, but I'd never gone swimming in it because we used the club or David Spencer's pool.)

Ralph was delighted that I could come. "I'll get the list and check off your name," he said.

He went inside and came back with a pencil in one hand and a notepad in the other. With a flourish of the pencil, he made a large check mark next to my name.

"Let's see now," he said, studying the pad. "So far we've had two nos and two yeses. Jamie and Meredith are the two nos. They're both going on vacation with their parents that week."

That would cut down on the girls and the little kids. Too bad, though. I kind of liked Meredith, and Jamie wasn't that much of a pest.

"Who's the other yes?"

"Kevin."

"Kevin Sherman?"

Ralph nodded.

I peered at him to see if he was kidding, but there wasn't a hint of a smile.

"I didn't know you and Kevin were friends," I said.

"Sure," Ralph said. "We've been in the same class since kindergarten, and his parents and my parents know each other from church. I always invite Kevin to my parties."

I let out a low whistle. This was going to be quite a party. A day at Playland plus a chance to show Kevin Sherman that I wasn't such a bad kid after all. Zow-*EE!* I could hardly wait for August 18th.

Ralph's party was the first good thing that had happened since we moved to Grossville, but it was two whole weeks away. I didn't think I could stand it. By a miracle, something turned up that made the waiting less of a drag. David Spencer's mother invited us over for lunch and a swim in their pool.

I knew it was Mrs. Spencer as soon as Mom answered the phone. "Sally," she burbled. "How nice to hear from you!"

There was a lot of chitchat back and forth, and then Mom said, "I'm sure they would. Yes, Tuesday is perfect. Fine. We'll look forward to seeing you."

Jenny and I knew "they" meant us, so we managed to be on hand when Mom hung up.

"How do you guys feel about spending a day in Glenville?" she said.

It sounded okay to me, but Jenny balked.

"Can I bring Pamela?" she asked.

"Pamela wasn't invited," Mom said. "Anyway, I don't think Beth would be very pleased if you brought another friend along."

Beth was David's little sister. She and Jenny weren't best friends like David and me, but they got along okay.

"Then I don't want to go," Jenny pouted.

"Stop acting like a baby," Mom said. "You and Pamela can survive a day apart. Besides, I've already accepted for all three of us."

That was the end of that.

I was looking forward to seeing David again, but I wasn't sure how the visit would go. When you haven't played with someone for a long time, you don't know if you'll still get along. I was the same, but David might have changed. Or now that we didn't see each other every day, we might not have anything to talk about.

I wondered if Mom had the same worry. She and Mrs. Spencer had been out of touch, too. They used to be tennis partners, but as far as I knew, Mom hadn't played tennis all summer. She was too busy getting our new house organized and studying the want ads in the newspapers. She was still talking about getting a job, but so far, nothing had turned up. I can't say that I was sorry.

The first thing that was different about visiting David Spencer was parking in the driveway and going up the front walk instead of cutting through the azalea bushes and knocking on the back door. The second thing was that Mrs. Spencer—not David—let us in. She gave all of us, including Mom, huge hugs. When David and Beth appeared, Mom hugged them. I could see that David didn't go for all that mushy stuff any more than I did, but we had to be polite.

Mrs. Spencer and Mom adjourned to the patio for a glass of white wine before lunch. Beth dragged Jenny off to organize a dolls' tea party, and David and I were left to fend for ourselves.

"How's it going?" I asked.

"Not bad," he answered.

There was an awkward pause while we both shuffled our feet and stared at the walls. David broke the silence. "Do you think the Yanks will ever get out of third place?" he said.

That got us going. In another minute, we were yakking back and forth about George Steinbrenner and Dave Winfield and arguing over which teams were going to make it to the World Series, just the way we used to. We got so absorbed in the discussion that Lydia, the Spencers' housekeeper, had to call us twice for lunch.

Mom and Mrs. Spencer were yakking away at a great rate, too. Mrs. Spencer seemed to be filling Mom in on the local gossip. As we walked into the dining room, I heard her saying, "They seem nice enough, but she certainly doesn't have your good taste. The living room is a disaster."

I knew they were talking about the people who'd bought our house. Later, when David and I were sitting beside the pool waiting for lunch to digest, I asked him if he played with the kids who lived there.

"They're the wrong ages," he said disgustedly. "The two boys are in high school and the girl goes to college."

"How's our old climbing tree?"

"I wish it were on our property instead of theirs," he grumbled. "It's the best climbing tree in Glenville, but nobody's gone near it since you moved away."

The two of us stared wistfully over at the tree that towered above the azalea bushes separating the two yards. In the stillness, I could hear a soft cooing sound coming from somewhere in the upper branches.

"Listen," I exclaimed. "Isn't that a mourning dove?"

"A what?"

"A mourning dove," I said. "Hear it? That low cooing sound."

David looked up.

"What's the big deal?" he said. "It's just some silly old pigeon."

"That's what I thought the first time I saw a mourning dove," I said. "But then Ralph pointed out that they're brown instead of grey, and if you get up close, you can see that they have a dark spot on the sides of their necks."

Maybe it was a show-offy thing to say, but I was proud of how much I'd learned about birds from hanging around with Ralph. I'll never be the expert he is, but I can recognize a few species, and I know a little bit about their habits.

David wasn't impressed with my lecture.

"Who's Ralph?" he demanded.

"He's this kid who lives near us in Humboldt. He knows an amazing amount about birds."

"Birds?"

David made a noise like he was about to barf.

"They're interesting," I said stoutly, "and Ralph's a nice guy. You'd like him."

"He sounds like a weirdo to me."

Before I could answer, David jumped up and dove into the pool. What the heck, I thought, we can argue about Ralph some other time. I did a cannonball that splashed a gallon of water in David's face. He retaliated by diving under and grabbing my ankles, almost dragging me off my feet.

I could have stayed there for the rest of the day, fooling around in the water and jumping off the diving board, but eventually I noticed that David and I had the pool to ourselves. Before long, Mom and Jenny reappeared in their going-home clothes, and Mom called to me to get changed, too.

"One more jump off the diving board," I begged. I took that plus an extra one, and then David and I padded inside to get dressed.

"Hey, that was fun," I said, trying to untangle my underwear from the rest of my clothes.

David gave a half-hearted grunt. I looked over and saw him glowering at me.

"What's the matter?" I said.

"How'd you get so friendly with that bird freak?" he snarled.

"Ralph?" I was surprised he was still brooding. "I don't know. He lives near me. Why?"

"What's his other name?"

"Kowalski."

"What kind of a name is that?"

"How should I know?" I said. "Anyway, he's a really nice kid. He's into birds because he can't play too many sports. He's got this disease called cystic fibrosis. . . ."

David had a sour expression on his face. I probably didn't look very happy either. I couldn't stand the way he was grilling me. If I wanted to be friends with Ralph, that was my business, not his. Of course I knew David didn't agree with me, and I also knew why.

When David and I hung out together in Glenville, he was always in charge. He decided what we'd do and who we'd play with, and I'd trail along in his wake. Now he was miffed because I'd gone ahead and done something on my own. Twice as miffed because it was something he'd never do. You wouldn't find David Spencer making friends with a kid who was a little bit different. No sir, not him. Kids like that were nerds or weirdos.

For the next few minutes, we both concentrated on getting dressed. David finished first. He came and stood over me as I was tying my sneakers. When I glanced up, I saw a nasty smirk on his face.

"I'm going to tell everyone in Glenville that Michael Bailey's new best friend is a birdbrain," he said.

If he thought I was going to keel over and die, he had another think coming.

"Bug off," I snarled.

David looked startled. He's always been good at thinking up cracks, and he can make life miserable for anyone he decides to pick on. But what did I care? I didn't live in Glenville anymore. I didn't have to be afraid of David Spencer's big mouth.

David wouldn't quit. "Doesn't it bother you to have a birdbrain for a best friend?" he snickered.

72

"He's not a birdbrain," I shouted. "And if you want to know something, he's a better friend than you are. He's not always trying to push me around and have things his own way!"

"Oh yeah? Well, at least I don't hang around with a kid who's got a name and a disease you can't pronounce."

That did it.

"You're a scumbag," I said.

"So are you."

I don't know who threw the first punch, but the next thing you know, the two of us were rolling around on the floor, pounding each other for all we were worth. Every time I socked David, he'd sock me right back. Nobody was winning and nobody was ready to give up.

"DAVID! MICHAEL! STOP THAT IMMEDIATELY!"

Mom and Mrs. Spencer must have come into the room while David and I were trying to slaughter each other on the floor. We stopped fighting and stood up. In the mirror over David's dresser, I could see that my face was streaked with sweat and my shirt was ripped at the shoulder. David didn't look much better.

"What's going on?" Mrs. Spencer wanted to know.

David and I stared down at the rug. "Nothing," we replied in unison.

Mrs. Spencer turned to Mom. "I'm awfully sorry," she said. "I don't know what got into David."

"I'm sure it wasn't all his fault," Mom replied, giving me an icy stare. "It takes two to start a fight."

As usual, each mother blamed her own kid. Mrs. Spencer blew up at David for being a bad host, and Mom blew up at me for being a bad guest. Then they made us shake hands and say we were sorry. We did as we were told, but

I wasn't sorry, and I could see that David wasn't either. Frankly, I didn't care if I ever saw him again, and I had a hunch he felt the same way about me.

The one thing I did want to see before we left Glenville was 28 Forest Road.

"I hope we're going to drive around the corner and take a look at our old house," I said as we got in the car and Mom started fishing for her keys.

"I've been trying to make up my mind about that."

She pulled the keys out of her purse and stuck them in the ignition, but she waited a second before turning on the engine. I heard her take the same kind of deep breath I always take to steel myself when the doctor is about to give me a shot.

"Okay," she said. "I'm game if you are. Let's do it."

Anyone who hadn't lived there would have said the house looked exactly the same, but I could tell right away that it was somebody else's turf. A gangly high school boy was standing out front, talking to a couple of kids in a silver Toyota. Another kid—the gangly one's brother, I suppose—was tossing a basketball through a hoop mounted above the garage door. I remembered Dad talking about putting up one of those for me; he had never gotten around to it.

Jenny stared out the car window and said, "Are we going to move back to that house, Mommy?"

Leave it to Jenny to miss the whole point!

"No," Mom told her. "It belongs to another family now. We just drove by to take a look at it."

Mom's voice cracked, and for a minute I thought she was going to cry. She pulled a tissue out of her purse and made a few quick swipes at her nose. When she started talking again, she sounded almost normal.

"The new family has really settled in," she said. "It looks as though they've been living there forever."

I'd been thinking the same thing. "I guess houses adjust to new people faster than people adjust to new houses," I said.

"I'm afraid you're right," Mom said.

Nobody talked until we got on the parkway back to Humboldt. Then Mom picked up the conversation as though there had never been a lull.

"We had some good times in that house," she said, "but we'll have some good times in our new house, too. Life will go on. We'll survive."

Mom sounded as if she were making that promise to herself as much as to Jenny and me.

"We're already surviving," I said.

That was an odd thing to come popping out of my mouth. Thinking positive has never been one of my strong points. What was even odder was that I wasn't just saying it to make Mom feel better; I really meant it.

In spite of my brawl with David Spencer, I was feeling good about life. And do you know something? I think the brawl was what did it. After years of being David Spencer's yes-man. I'd finally gotten up the nerve to stand on my own two feet.

I turned to look out the back window, but Glenville had long since disappeared behind the curves of concrete. The Grossville exit was coming up fast. That didn't make me feel as glum as it should have. I know I'll never stop missing Glenville, but moving to Grossville wasn't all bad.

I was surviving, wasn't I? And I was learning a few things besides. One of them was that only a bossy, opinionated snob like David Spencer needs a big house and a classy neighborhood to prove he's worth something. All I need is myself.

Ralph's birthday party seemed like ages away when he invited me. But all of a sudden I woke up one morning and *pow!*—it was August 18th.

I had to rummage through my dresser drawers to find a shirt without an alligator that still looked okay. Step one for making a good impression on Kevin.

Mom did a double take when I came down for breakfast. "I haven't seen that shirt in ages," she said. "I'd written it off as lost, strayed, or stolen."

"It was right there in my dresser drawer," I informed her smugly. I figured I had a right to be smug; it was the first time in my life that I knew where something was and she didn't.

Jenny was chowing down on cereal and bananas, and

prattling away about some jump-rope contest in which she and Pamela had trounced two other little girls. You'd think they'd won the Superbowl the way she was carrying on about it. I grunted now and again to make it look like I was listening, but my mind was on Ralph's party.

I wondered how the Kowalskis would work it. Taking a gang of kids to Playland is no easy job. The swimming wouldn't be so bad, but the party was bound to come unglued when it came time to go on the rides. Nobody ever likes the same ones. There's always someone who loves the Whip and hates the ferris wheel and vice versa, and someone else who's too chicken to go on anything but the kiddy rides. Oh well, that was the Kowalskis' problem.

Mine was Kevin Sherman. What could I do to convince him that I was a good kid and we ought to be friends? I had no idea, but I couldn't resist running through a few possibilities. One—my favorite—starred me doing something spectacular, like executing a perfect swan dive off the thirty-foot board or scoring a thousand at Skeeball. Kevin would come up to me with an awed look and say, "That was fantastic. I hope there's no hard feelings. I'd consider it an honor if we could be friends."

There was always the possibility, though, that Kevin and I would go our separate ways. With a bunch of kids, I could see how it might happen. He'd team up with the ones he knew, I'd team up with the ones I knew, and we'd never say a word to each other. If things worked out that way, I was sunk. I might never have another shot at extricating myself from the fun-and-games crowd in Ralph's backyard and joining the jocks at the Woodycrest School playground.

I arrived at Ralph's house precisely at 9 A.M. Three or four kids were there ahead of me, clutching the bags and knapsacks that held their swimming gear. Another gang trooped in behind me. The presents were being stacked on the floor in front of the TV set, so we added ours to the pile.

I knew a lot of the kids from hanging out at Ralph's. He introduced me to the rest. I also met Mr. Kowalski, who had taken the day off to help with the party. He had a friendly grin, just like Ralph's.

"Oh yes, you're the one who moved here from Glenville," he said when he heard my name.

The living room was getting crowded, so we went outside and milled around on the sidewalk. Mrs. Kowalski counted heads for the third time and came up with eleven.

"There are supposed to be twelve," she said. "Who's missing?"

"Kevin," Ralph told her.

"He's definitely coming," somebody volunteered. "I talked to him last night."

"Maybe he overslept," Ralph's mother said. "Why don't we wait in the cars?"

The Kowalskis had borrowed a van from Ralph's uncle. That held eight kids plus Mr. Kowalski, who was going to drive. Ralph's mother was taking the other four in the Kowalskis' Chevy.

I had already climbed into the van and grabbed a seat by the window when Kevin came running up. Would you believe it—he was wearing an alligator shirt? The van was already full, so Kevin had to go in the car. I saw him climb in the backseat and deliver a couple of crampers to the two kids who were already there. I thought those two looked familiar. Now I realized that they were two-thirds of Kevin's goon squad.

My hopes took a nosedive. That could be the beginning of my Separate Ways scenario. Or was I being negative again? I looked around at the van full of kids and ordered myself to think positive. How bad can anything be when you're on your way to Playland?

To keep us from getting antsy, Ralph's father suggested a game of Ghost. One kid—an airhead named Allen— couldn't get the hang of it. He was so proud of himself every time he came up with the letter that made a word. He couldn't get it through his skull that the object was to avoid doing that. By the time he caught on, he'd already lost.

As we were pulling into the Playland parking lot, Ralph's father gave us a rundown on the day's schedule. "Swimming first, then lunch," he said. "After that, we'll go on a few rides. Then back to our house for cake and ice cream while Ralph opens his presents."

"All *right!*" we yelled in unison. We scrambled out of the van and collided with the kids who had ridden over in the car. They had pulled into the parking lot behind us and parked only two stalls away.

"First stop is the pool," Ralph's father reminded everyone. "And remember, stick together. We don't want to lose anyone."

I stuck with the two kids, John and Tommy, who had shared my seat in the van. Kevin got lost in the crowd. The next time I saw him we were making our way through the showers and footbaths you have to walk through before they'll let you into the pool. We emerged at the same time and headed straight for the deep end of the pool.

I'd planned to dive right in and show Kevin what an expert swimmer I am, but a gang of older kids—they looked to be about thirteen or so—had taken over the entire nine-foot end of the pool. One kid was sitting in a small blue plastic boat, and his friends were trying to dump him out. The four of them were having a wild time, whooping and splashing and yelling insults at each other. They must have known they were hogging the deep water, but their attitude was, So what?

Kevin and I stopped at the edge of the pool. He looked at me as if to say, "What do we do now?"

I didn't know either. We stood there for another minute before the lifeguard came to our rescue. With a sharp blast of his whistle, he motioned to the older kids.

"Okay, you guys," he shouted. "Break up the game and give the other folks a chance to swim."

The lifeguard wasn't the type you argued with. The kid in the plastic boat immediately made his way over to the side of the pool and tried to climb out. Before he could manage it, one of his friends sneaked up behind him and tipped the boat over. It looked like a new round of whooping and splashing might begin, but the lifeguard cut it short. He gave another blast on his whistle, and the whole crew scrambled out of the pool, dragging the boat behind them.

Kevin and I dove in and started swimming around. We were the only kids from Ralph's party at the nine-foot end of the pool. The rest of them were doggy-paddling around in the shallow water.

Kevin took a dive off the board, and I went off behind him. We weren't actually talking to each other, but we were edging up to it. I swam over to the side of the pool, expecting to scramble up the metal ladder and take another dive, but one of the kids who'd been hogging the pool when we got there was blocking the way. When I reached over to grab one of the handrails, he shoved my arm aside.

"The lifeguard broke up our little game on account of you and your pal," he said, flicking some water in my face. "But don't worry, we've found a new game to play."

I already knew the name of it: Torture the Younger Kids.

I looked over and saw that one of the other pool hogs was keeping Kevin off the ladder on the opposite side of the pool. Kevin swam around him and tried to hoist himself up along the side. But another member of the gang appeared and stood in his way. The fourth pool hog was standing on my side of the pool, waiting to do the same thing to me.

I thought of swimming straight down to the shallow end of the pool, but I knew if I tried it, the kid at the ladder would abandon his post and cut me off. He was bigger and stronger than I was. I could never outswim him.

By now, I was treading water like crazy, wondering how much longer this game was going to last. On the opposite side of the pool, Kevin seemed to be doing the same thing.

The scariest part of it all was that no one could tell what was happening. Unless they studied the situation closely, they'd never know that those big kids had us trapped, or that Kevin and I weren't treading water because we liked to.

My arms and legs were getting tired. I didn't want to be chicken and scream for help, but if I waited too much longer, I might not have any breath left.

Suddenly I heard Ralph's voice. "Kevin! Michael!" he was yelling. "Come on out of the water. I want to see you dive."

I turned my head in the direction of the sound. Ralph was stretched out on the diving board on his stomach, peering down at the two of us in the water. Neither Kevin nor I could answer him. We were too busy trying to keep our heads above water and not swallow half the pool.

"Kevin! Michael!" Ralph yelled again. "Did you hear me?"

Ralph couldn't figure out why we didn't respond. Then he looked over and saw the kids at the ladders. It only took him a second to size up the situation. He jumped up and raced over to the lifeguard stand. In another second, the lifeguard leaped down from his perch, and began blowing his whistle non-stop.

The two bullies on the edge of the pool darted off in the direction of the bathhouse. The two in the water climbed out and ran after them. Kevin and I made a lunge for the ladders and clung to them until we caught our breath.

As soon as we recovered, we climbed out and joined Ralph on a bench near the diving board.

"Thank goodness you've got sharp eyes," I told him. "That was pretty hairy."

"It sure was," Kevin agreed. "What a bunch of rats! I hope the lifeguard gives it to them good."

The lifeguard had rounded up the four bullies near the

entrance to the pool, and it looked like that's what he was doing.

By the time we went back in the water, Kevin and I were talking to each other as if we'd never been on the brink of World War III. We compared notes on how we felt when the bullies blocked our way out of the pool, and our answers were the same: scared. We discussed what we'd do if we met them again and agreed on that one, too: call for help right away.

When Mr. and Mrs. Kowalski rounded us up for lunch, we walked back to the bathhouse together. It struck me that Kevin didn't seem as tall as he had when we first met. He couldn't have shrunk, so I must have grown.

Ralph's parents had brought two huge coolers full of fruit and sandwiches and an endless supply of lemonade. We ate in the picnic area with Kevin and me sitting side by side at one of the tables. The kid opposite us, Richie, mentioned something about tennis lessons. I gathered that he and Kevin were enrolled in a class at the public courts near the high school.

"Is it too late to sign up?" I asked, thinking of how pleased Dad would be if I took up tennis again.

" 'Fraid so," Kevin said. "The classes end in another week."

I shrugged as if it didn't matter that much. "Maybe next summer," I said.

After lunch, Ralph's father gave us the game plan for the rest of the afternoon. Waving a fistful of scrip tickets that were good on all the rides, he proceeded to dole them out. "You can spend them wherever you like," he said. "The only rule is that you have to let us know where you'll be."

Kevin and I went on all the scary rides.

"You guys sure have guts," Ralph grinned when we came bouncing off the Dragon Coaster after our second trip. "Once was enough for me."

The three of us checked our supply of scrip tickets and realized that we each had enough for one more ride.

"Let's go on one together," Kevin suggested.

"Good idea," I said. "Which one?"

Kevin turned to Ralph.

"It's your party. You pick it."

"The merry-go-round," Ralph said without a second's hesitation.

The merry-go-round has always been my idea of the Wimp Special, but who was I to argue with my host? The three of us sauntered over to the merry-go-round. We arrived just as it stopped, so we had our pick of the horses. "Get one on the outside," Ralph told us. "Then we can try for the rings."

The last time I'd been on the merry-go-round was when I was six years old; nobody had told me about the rings. When Kevin and I had both mounted our outside horses, I called over to Ralph, "Where are the rings?"

"Over there." He pointed to a funny-looking contraption on the other side of the shed. "Wrap your arm around the brass pole and lean out as far as you can."

The calliope began wheezing, and the merry-go-round started up. As the scenery whizzed past, I heard Ralph yell, "Gotcha!"

He had hooked his finger through a ring on his very first try. I stretched out my arm but missed.

"Rats!" The exclamation came from Kevin, who was on the horse behind me. He must have missed, too.

"Lean out farther the next time," Ralph yelled to us both.

I did as I was told and—zap!—my index finger went through the ring. I could hear a click as another ring dropped in its place.

"Rats!" exclaimed the voice behind me again. I guess Kevin still hadn't gotten the hang of it.

We whirled around with the music blaring in our ears. I was having such a good time lunging for the rings that I felt cheated when the ride was over. To tell you the truth, I never knew the merry-go-round could be such fun. If my scrip tickets weren't all used up, I would have gone on it again.

One of the attendants was standing by the exit to collect the rings we had grabbed. Kevin and I had two each. Ralph had seven.

"We gave you a break because it's your birthday," Kevin told him.

"I'll bet," he said.

We found Ralph's parents standing in front of a frozen custard stand surrounded by a cluster of disheveled kids.

"Here come the three stragglers," Ralph's mother said. "Time to be on our way."

The party ended at Ralph's house. He opened his presents at the dining-room table, and we all sang "Happy Birthday" while he blew out the candles and cut the cake.

"Which way are you heading?" Kevin asked when it was time to go home.

I pointed in the direction of our house.

"Me too," he said. "I'll walk you."

"That was some party," I remarked as we strolled along together.

Kevin nodded. "Ralph's parents always go all-out."

After a few minutes Kevin said, "Did you watch the Yankee–White Sox game last night?"

"I wish I hadn't," I said mournfully. "The Yanks blew it. They never should have put in a relief pitcher."

"That's exactly what I thought."

We came to our house first. "This is where I live," I announced.

Kevin nodded. "My house is down there on the corner of Maple Avenue."

As if I didn't know.

"A bunch of us are having a pickup game at the school playground tomorrow morning," Kevin said. "Why don't you stop by?"

"Sounds good."

"Great. See you tomorrow."

I lingered on the sidewalk for an extra few minutes, watching my new friend head on down the street. On the next block, he turned and gave me a farewell wave. Then he disappeared behind the same hedges where, only a few weeks before, he'd threatened to beat me up and steal my bike.

I had a few twinges of guilt about abandoning Ralph and teaming up with Kevin. You couldn't do that sort of thing in Glenville without causing a big flap; but as far as I could tell, Ralph didn't mind at all. Maybe he didn't have to be possessive about one friend because he had so many others.

If anything, Ralph acted pleased that Kevin and I had gotten together.

"I always knew you two would make a good pair," he said one afternoon when we dropped by on our way home from the school playground.

There was something about the way he said it that made me wonder if he'd planned his birthday party with that in mind. He didn't arrange for the pool hogs, of course, but I think Kevin and I would have signed a truce that day even if we hadn't almost drowned.

Kevin and I did make a good pair. We became best friends the day after Ralph's party, and since then we've been as inseparable as Jenny and Pamela.

Before long, Mom was complaining that she'd forgotten what I looked like. I'd zoom off to meet Kevin at the playground the instant I'd finished breakfast and made my bed. Mom was sticking to her guns on the bedmaking. She wouldn't take over no matter how bad a job I did. Every once in a while she'd come into my room and shake her head, but her only comment was, "It's your bed, as the saying goes, you're the one who has to lie in it. Still, I can't believe it's very comfortable."

It wouldn't have been for her. The bedspread was always lumpy, and the sheets were never straight, but I didn't have any trouble getting to sleep.

"I suppose not," Mom said. "Considering the amount of running around you do, you must be shattered by bedtime. It's a wonder you have the strength to climb the stairs."

Kevin and I spent most of our time playing soccer or softball with the other jocks in the neighborhood. Occasionally, the two of us would cut out for a game of tennis. He was a good player, but I was better because I'd been playing longer. When I saw how much he disliked being beaten all the time, I suggested that we volley instead of playing games, so he could practice his strokes.

"What a nice thing to do," Mom said after I explained why the answer was "nobody" when she asked who'd won.

I could feel my ears turning red. It's not often that I get commended for doing nice things. Maybe it's because it's not often that I do any.

Hanging around with Kevin left me no time for cooking or snacking or even eating my regular meals.

"What's the rush? Take your time," Mom would say as I stuffed a forkful of hamburger into my mouth.

"Can't," I'd say. "We have to finish the game before it gets dark."

I was wolfing down my cereal at the same breakneck speed one morning when Mom said, "I've got an idea. . . ."

I immediately put all systems on full alert.

"Yes?" I said warily.

"We ought to return the Spencers' invitation before the summer's over."

A zero-minus idea if I'd ever heard one.

"Why?"

"For openers, it's the polite thing to do," she said. "But it would also be nice to see them again, and I know they'd like to see our new house."

I couldn't imagine why. It was tacky compared to the houses in Glenville. I was positive David would go back and tell all my old friends that I was living in Barf Manor.

Not only that, it would mean giving up playing with Kevin for a day.

"You don't look very enthusiastic about the idea," Mom said.

"I'm not. I hate David Spencer. I don't care if I ever see him again."

"But you used to be best friends," Mom said. "What happened?"

"I'm sick of him," I said. "He's too bossy. He wants all his friends to do things his way."

"Is that all?"

"No."

"What else?"

"He said some rotten things about Ralph Kowalski."

"Such as?"

"He called him a birdbrain. . . ."

"And?"

"He said he had a name and a disease you couldn't pronounce."

"That's rotten, all right," Mom agreed.

We both sat there staring down at the table for a few minutes.

"Is that what started the fight that day we went over to Glenville?" Mom asked.

I nodded.

"Hmmmm." Mom shifted around in her chair. "Hmmmm," she said again. "Did it ever occur to you that David might be jealous of Ralph?"

"Why?"

"For taking his place as your friend."

"But David's got plenty of other kids to play with," I protested. "Back then, I only had Ralph."

"That's true," Mom said. "But you and David were very special friends. And you have to remember that David's never moved to a new town. He doesn't know how difficult it is to make friends."

"I could tell him," I muttered. I thought about David for a while. We'd had a lot of fun together; maybe I shouldn't let one nasty crack come between us.

"I suppose I don't really hate him," I said to Mom. "But I still don't want to have him over."

"Any special reason?"

There was no point in beating around the bush. "I don't want him to see this house."

"What's wrong with it?" Mom said, as if she honestly didn't know and was hoping I could tell her.

"The whole place would fit inside the Spencers' living room," I said. "And if they come for lunch, we'll have to eat in that stupid dining area instead of a real dining room, and there won't be a pool to go swimming in—" I stopped abruptly. Running down the list of all the things that were wrong with our house made me want to cry. Not because the place was that bad—actually, I'd gotten used to it—but because talking about it reminded me of Glenville and the divorce and the way things used to be.

Mom took a deep breath. "I know exactly how you feel, believe me," she said. "Why do you think it's taken me so long to get around to doing this?"

That was a shock. Mom usually acted as though moving to Grossville was an adventure instead of a disaster.

"But, you know, Michael," she went on, "this may not be a mansion, but it's neat and clean and attractively furnished. And, even more important, it's *ours*."

"What does that mean?"

"It means that if people care about us, they're not going to worry about where we live or how much money we have. They're going to look at the important things, like whether we're honest and thoughtful, and how we treat the people we deal with every day."

Mom was making a speech, but what she was saying

made sense. Ralph's house wasn't as nicely furnished as ours, but he was one of the neatest kids I'd ever met. Then there was Kevin, my best friend and constant companion. His parents didn't go tripping off to the Caribbean or talk about their wine cellar the way the Spencers did. And yet I enjoyed his company as much as I'd ever enjoyed David's. I had to concede that Mom had a point, but that didn't mean that everyone else felt the same way. As usual, Mom came up with an answer to that one, too.

"Well, if other people's values are scrambled, that's their problem, not yours," she said.

"That's easy for you to say," I grumbled. "Grown-ups don't make snotty remarks to people's faces. Kids are meaner."

"I know," Mom said. "But let's look at it another way. Are you the same person you were when we lived in Glenville?"

"That's a dumb question. Sure."

"So if somebody who knew and liked you then makes a snotty remark about you now, doesn't that prove that his head is on backwards?"

"All right, you win," I said. "But I still don't want to deal with any stuck up kid from Glenville."

"Listen," Mom said sternly. "This is a two-way street. It's just as mindless for you to dump on people who live in Glenville as it is for them to dump on people who live in Humboldt."

"Okay, okay. I get the message," I said. "Why did you ask me? You're obviously going to invite the Spencers no matter what I say."

"I'm going to invite Mrs. Spencer, but if you and Jenny

don't want to see David and Beth, I'll make up some excuse. Why don't you think it over and let me know what you decide?"

I thought about it on and off for the rest of the day. Our house was no great shakes, but Mom had fixed it up so it didn't look too bad. And I knew lunch would be all right, even without a dining room to eat in. Although she sometimes goes overboard on foods that are Good For You, generally speaking, Mom is a terrific cook.

Okay. I could get through that part of it, but how would I entertain David for the afternoon? Maybe that wouldn't be such a problem either. David loves softball, but in Glenville it's always hard to scare up enough guys for a game. That was no sweat here. Kevin and I could easily round up two teams. And I wouldn't have to skip playing with him that day, after all.

"When you call Mrs. Spencer, tell her to bring David," I told Mom at dinner that night. "He's traveled everywhere else in the country. He might as well see Grossville."

"Humboldt," Mom corrected me. "When are you going to stop calling it Grossville."

"When it stops being gross," I said.

"When will that be?"

"Who knows? Maybe never."

Mom called Mrs. Spencer and made a date for the following Thursday; Jenny had already agreed to invite Beth. I was praying something would happen so they wouldn't be able to come, but nothing did. Thursday arrived, and there they were on our doorstep.

Mrs. Spencer oohed and ahed over the way Mom had

decorated the house. She also loved the cold chicken curry Mom made for lunch.

"How I envy your talents as a cook!" she exclaimed. "If we didn't have Lydia, we'd never have an edible meal."

David and I got along fine. I'd like to believe it was because I was such an excellent host, but I think it was because that brawl we'd had in Glenville was too far back to worry about. Or maybe we were both in a good mood because the Yankees were having a winning streak.

After we ate, Mom and Mrs. Spencer settled down for a gabfest. Jenny dragged Beth off to Pamela's house, and David and I headed for the school playground where Kevin and some of the other guys were waiting for us.

I introduced David all around and we chose up sides for the game. Amazingly, all three of us got on the same team. A couple of hours later I was hanging around behind home plate, waiting for my turn at bat, when I heard the beep of a horn. I looked across the ball field and saw Mrs. Spencer waving from her car.

"Tell David to get over here," she called. "It's time to go home."

David, who had just hit a single and was safely ensconced on first base, saw her, too. He called time-out and raced over to the curb.

"Just a few more minutes, please," he begged. "The score's tied. This is the last half of the last inning, and we've got two outs and two men on base."

Mrs. Spencer sighed and shut off the engine.

"Okay, but I'm warning you, if it goes into extra innings, you can't stay. We're late as it is."

David tore back across the field to his position on first

base. I was the next one up. Chris, the pitcher, had a wicked curve. I swung at two of them and missed by a foot and a half, but on the next pitch, I heard a beautiful *whumpf* as the bat connected with the ball. I went racing toward first and kept on going to second. Kevin, who had been on second, was rounding third with David right behind. I loped in behind him and our whole team started jumping up and down and cheering like a bunch of maniacs. The final score was 6–3, and the other team was still combing the bushes for the ball.

When the excitement died down, I walked over to the car with David.

"What a fantastic game we had!" he said to his mother. "I wish we lived around here so I could play with these guys every day."

I don't think Mrs. Spencer was about to move to Grossville, but she was glad to hear that David had enjoyed himself.

"Maybe Michael will invite you over again," she said.

"Sure," I promised. "Why not?"

Mom was putting away the last of the lunch dishes when I got home.

"Did everything go all right between you and David?" she asked.

"I'll say!" I exclaimed. "He can hardly wait to be invited back."

"Good," Mom said.

You don't know how relieved I was that it wasn't, "I told you so."

"What's for dinner?" I asked.

"We've all had a busy day," Mom said. "I thought we might eat at McDonald's."

"Sounds good," I said. "Would you like me to empty the garbage before we leave?"

It was one of the few times in my life I'd volunteered to be helpful, but if Mom noticed it, she didn't let on.

"That would be very nice," she said. "Thank you."

I knew summer was coming to an end when the stores in the shopping center started advertising back-to-school specials on everything from pencil cases to peanut butter.

"When does school start?" Dad asked us one Sunday toward the end of August.

I didn't know, but Jenny had the date on the tip of her tongue.

"September seventh," she said. Pamela must have told her.

"Only two more weeks to live," Dad said.

I don't know why grown-ups always assume that you hate to go back to school. In some ways, I wasn't crazy about the idea, but at the same time, I was itching to find out what sixth grade would be like.

If you want to know the truth, what bothers me more than starting school is the last-minute hassle of buying new clothes and getting my hair cut and going to the doctor for a checkup. It uses up the last few free days, and it's boring besides.

Our Sunday visits with Dad weren't a big production anymore. We'd all agreed that getting together every second week was enough, and Dad stopped preparing minute-by-minute plans of our day's activities. We rented bikes or went to the movies or a museum if we felt like it, but sometimes we just wandered around town gawking at the sights.

Dad also cut down on our restaurant-going and started feeding us at his apartment.

"I like it better," Jenny confided to me. "You can see what you're getting before some waiter plonks it down in front of you."

I'm more of a restaurant freak than Jenny is, but I thought it was better, too. This way, you could ask for seconds.

Dad's neighborhood was full of different kinds of food stores, so on top of the old standbys, like steak and spaghetti, he often gave us new dishes to try. I don't usually like strange foods, but the ones Dad picked out weren't bad.

Jenny was the table setter and salad tosser for our Sunday night suppers, and Dad and I handled the cooking. It was a relief to discover that he wasn't as bad as he'd claimed to be. Since I wasn't as good as I'd claimed to be, it worked out fine.

"What new recipes did you try this time?" Mom asked

99

one Monday morning after we'd spent the previous day with Dad.

I told her about a Greek dish called *pastitso*. It tasted a little bit like lasagne, and although it took a long time to make, it was definitely worth it.

Mom was on the verge of asking what was in it when the telephone rang. Instead of taking the call in the kitchen, she ran upstairs to her bedroom. When she came back down, she had a funny smile on her face.

Mom had just gotten the word that she was being hired for the training program at some computer company that had its offices in Humboldt. I shouldn't have been so stunned. She'd been poring over the want ads for weeks, and the refrigerator door was festooned with the addresses and phone numbers of places she was going for job interviews.

Actually, I wasn't stunned so much as upset at the idea of Mom going to work. Who was going to take care of me and Jenny if we got sick and had to stay home from school?

"Don't worry. We'll work something out," Mom promised.

The more pressing problem, Mom said, was how she was going to manage the housework and cooking. "I'll have to rely on you and Jenny," she said. "You already make your own beds; that's been a big help. Now you'll have to branch out to other chores. Jenny, you're old enough to do some dusting and sort the laundry. Michael, I'm hoping you'll lend a hand in the kitchen."

"What do you want me to do?" I asked warily.

"Nothing too complicated," Mom assured me. "Turn

100

on the oven and pop in a casserole, wash the salad greens and make the dressing—stuff like that."

It sounded easy enough, but wouldn't it cut into my playing time?

"To some extent," Mom admitted. "But we all have to make sacrifices for the common good."

Mom wasn't starting work until the week after we went back to school, so I didn't have to worry about making sacrifices just yet. I could concentrate on getting used to being in a new grade and a new school.

I wasn't as uptight about the new school as I thought I'd be. I'd spent most of the summer listening to other kids talk about the place, so I already knew which teachers were okay and which ones weren't, and what to expect of lunches and assemblies.

Kevin and I were praying we'd be assigned to the same sixth grade. "If you're not with me, you might be with Ralph," he said, "and the two sixth grades have sports together, so we'll see each other then."

"What does Ralph do about sports?" I asked.

"He's excused because of that sickness he's got," Kevin said. "He's allowed to sit and watch, but most of the time he goes to the library and reads."

"What a bummer," I said. "There was a kid in Glenville who had to wear a brace on his leg. The phys ed teacher made him the athletic manager. He took attendance and kept track of the schedules and equipment."

"That's a neat idea!" Kevin said. "Why don't we ask our phys ed teacher, Mr. Driscoll, to do that with Ralph?"

"Why don't *you* ask him?" I said. "I don't even know him."

"Okay," Kevin agreed. "But you come along and back me up."

"All right," I said. "But I don't see how anyone could object to the idea."

Kevin shrugged. "Sometimes people get used to doing things a certain way and they think it's the end of the world if they have to change."

"Right."

I don't know how much Kevin knew about changes, but I could have told him a thing or two. Some of them do seem like the end of the world, but if you hang in and think positive, eventually they work themselves out.

I never know what to do the night before school opens. You feel like you want to go out and play while you still can, but you also feel that you ought to stay home and do something to get ready for school. The only trouble is that aside from laying out your school clothes and sharpening a few pencils, there isn't an awful lot you can do.

"I'd better set the alarm," Mom said. "You don't want to be late on the very first day."

"I *can't* be late," Jenny declared. "Pamela is going to call for me at eight-fifteen sharp. She'll be mad if I'm not ready."

"And I'm meeting Kevin and Ralph and some of the other guys at the corner," I said. "We're going to walk to school together."

"I'll set the alarm for seven," Mom said. "That will give us plenty of time."

Mom shooed Jenny upstairs to take her bath and get ready for bed. I had another hour to go, so I turned on the Yankee game. Toward the end of the third inning, Mom came back from tucking Jenny in and kissing her good-night. When she saw that nothing much was happening on the TV screen, she sat down and struck up a conversation.

"How does it feel to be going to a new school?"

"I think I can handle it," I said.

"After all the other things you've handled this summer, this one ought to be a breeze," she said.

I nodded.

"I hope it hasn't been too awful for you," Mom went on in a more serious tone. "Your father and I hated to yank you and Jenny out of Glenville. We felt like we were making you suffer for something that wasn't your fault."

Only a few weeks ago, I would have shouted, "YOU WERE!" Now I let it pass. Mom already felt guilty—why make it worse?

I'd been having some long thoughts about the divorce, and I was beginning to put things together. The way I looked at it, we'd all been involved in a dreadful car wreck, but instead of being killed or crippled for life, we'd escaped with some broken bones and a few cuts and bruises. They hurt, no question about it, but the pain was beginning to let up, and with any luck, it would soon disappear. I suppose there'd be a few scars, but I could live with those, especially since I was fairly sure they wouldn't show.

I didn't try to explain all that to Mom. All I said was, "Glenville was a neat place to live, but we're doing okay in Humboldt."

Mom gave me a quick hug, then she pulled back and stared at me in amazement.

103

"Did I hear that right?"

"What?"

"You said Humboldt instead of Grossville."

"So?" I said, playing it cool so she wouldn't know that I'd surprised myself, too. "Isn't that what this town is called?"